"A lyric, tragic song of the road! An historic movie! A loose, lovely-to-look-at, often laughing, often lyric epic . . . in vivid contemporary terms. The film has a marvelous quality of being alive to its own possibilities and to the possibilities, good and bad, of the land it moves across." —Richard Schickel, LIFE

"A bold, courageous statement of life seldom matched in motion pictures! I couldn't shake what I'd seen, even after I left the theater." —Rex Reed

"EASY RIDER reached out and profoundly shook me! An eloquent, important movie!" —Joseph Morgenstern, NEWSWEEK

"One of the most powerful movies I've ever seen . . . one of the very few that doesn't cop out!" —THE VILLAGE VOICE

"EASY RIDER is the real thing! . . . Very alert, humorous, beautiful and modestly put. EASY RIDER speaks tersely and aptly for this American age that is both the best of times and the worst of times." —Penelope Gilliatt, THE NEW YORKER

Other SIGNET Film Books

☐ **SALESMAN—A Film by the Maysles Brothers and Charlotte Zwerin.** This first volume in the Signet Film Series contains a long interview with the Maysles plus an analysis of their unique approach to film-making, in addition to the script and stills of their much-heralded movie. (#Y3966—$1.25)

Watch for These
Forthcoming SIGNET Film Books

HOW STANLEY KUBRICK MADE 2001 by Jerome Agel
SCIENCE FICTION FILMS by Marilyn Goldin
ROLLING: Films Seen Through the Camera's Eye by Leo Garen
FACES by John Cassavetes

Easy Rider

Original screenplay by
PETER FONDA
DENNIS HOPPER
TERRY SOUTHERN

plus stills, interviews and articles

Edited by Nancy Hardin
and Marilyn Schlossberg

A SIGNET BOOK from
NEW AMERICAN LIBRARY
TIMES MIRROR

Acknowledgments

"Will *Easy* Do It for Dennis Hopper?" by Tom Burke appeared in *The New York Times* on July 20, 1969. © 1969 by The New York Times Company. Reprinted by permission.

"Jack Nicholson—Talking and Talked about" by Marjory Adams appeared in *The Boston Globe* on August 19, 1969. Reprinted by permission of Marjory Adams and *The Boston Globe*.

Easy Rider's Soundtrack by Robert Christgau is reprinted by permission of Robert Christgau % International Famous Agency, Inc., copyrighted by The Village Voice, Inc. 1969.

Rolling Stone Raps with Peter Fonda by Elizabeth Campbell. © 1969 by *Rolling Stone Magazine.* All rights reserved.

Introduction to *Easy Rider* by Frederic Tuten. Originally appeared in somewhat different form in *Film Society Review*, Vol. 4, No. 9, May, 1969. Reprinted by permission of the author.

Photographs by Peter Sorel.

Contents

Into the Issue of the Good Old Time Movie Versus the Good Old Time

In October of 1965 a national magazine asked me to write an article about movies. They turned down the article because they felt it was "an apologia for bad American movies" when what they had wanted was "a swinging piece explaining the young, bright types who are nuts about movie-going."

When I sat down to write something for this book I found that I was still as bitter as I was back in '65, so I'm giving you that article with only one change—a p.s. thanking Easy Rider's *angels.*

"Howdy! Rope 'em up." "Cut!" No good. Airplane. No good for sound. Airplane's gone. Good for sound. Roll 'em. Rolling speed. Buzzer. Clap board. Take six. Bang clank. Powder puff. Action. Dialogue. "Howdy! Rope 'em up."

(Cowboy throws rope out of frame. Director says "Cut! How'd it look?" Cameraman shrugs disinterestedly, shows us his shoulder. "It was all right." Shrugs again. Director: "Just all right?" Cameraman: "Mmm. It was good." Director: "Come on, man! How was it? Was it just good? The

by DENNIS HOPPER

7

loop in the lasso—I mean did it make a circle? Did you see it go out of frame?" Cameraman: "Yeah, I saw it. Yeah it was—it was fine." Soundman yells: "It was good for sound!" The director decides it was great, it wasn't just good, it was WHAM BAM right on the MONEY! It was great with a CAPITAL G! "Gee whiz!" says the little newspaper boy, "Shazam and no Captain Marvel?" and a great silence prevails, over dead water waiting for a waterfall.)

Movies are better than ever! Combining Good Citizenship With Good Movie-Making! Million-dollar low-budget fiasco, the million dollar baby!

"Fifteen million? What'd it gross?"

"I don't know."

"Must have made money, they're planning a twenty-five million dollar one."

"Let's hope so. Tours are our best seller this season. Kept us alive all summer. Yeah, they're no fools."

No. Well who is? And who needs Disneyland-with-glass-sound-stages-so-people-can-watch Studios? Props? Heavy equipment? Thirty people on a crew? Three dollars and seventy-five cents an hour for an old man who opens a door and sweeps cigarette butts off the floor and makes coffee (as a matter of fact great coffee), and when he dies (and believe me, he won't quit before), his son will take over and do the chore of opening and closing the door.

Big old-fashioned sound stages that cost them more to run and build sets on when the whole damn country's one big real place to utilize and film, and God's a great gaffer. Shoot natural light! Use lightweight reflectors!

"Bergman makes films with six on a crew. Wouldn't you?"

The talk goes on and on, but it's only a matter of time until somebody's going to do it. When it's only a matter of time, being patient helps. And I don't mean a patient like in a nuthouse.

Five years ago [in 1960—Ed. Note] there were fifty art theaters in the United States; now there are six thousand.

"They don't make money, those European films." Another Exec: "Yeah, you should see the bad ones."

Someone's smart over there in Europe. "America's where the money is," someone said about ten years ago. "How can we get into their market? We cannot compete on their level of film. Hey! I've got a great idea! Let's make art films. That's something they'll never think of!"

And of course we haven't yet.
Fifty theaters to six thousand in five years.
No American films for six thousand theaters.

"Oh well! Hmmm. You should see the bad ones."

The American Art Film cannot be an imitation of the European Art Film. Simple enough statement. Yes, it's simple enough, that statement. What's the answer? What's the question?

Bruce Connor, of all the so-called "underground moviemakers," is the most original talent. Bruce rarely shoots the film he edits. He takes quick cuts from many old movies and by juxtaposing them he makes much-more-than-interesting things happen. What a great idea for a major company to hire Connor. Turn him loose on the stockpile of films that lie decaying in the vaults of all the major studios, and make fresh films without the expense of shooting one foot of film. That's a multi-million-dollar idea. Have *you* had one lately?

The Sixteen Millimeter Film. The Sixteen Millimeter Film. Drinks flow. More talk into the night. More talk into the morning. More talk. Etcetera. Etcetera. Etcetera.

The Sixteen Millimeter Film Revolution. Is it possible? Oh, yes, it's absolutely possible. Oh, yes, honestly, it is absolutely possible. But not this way.

Cocktail   Gingerale   Five Cents A Glass
Ring Around The Rosey   Pocket Full Of Posey

A drag-down-around-the-corner approach to the cinema-come-lately American art film better known as the New American Film Society and still Better Known in the In Harper's Bazaar Vogue Top Top Top Mags as the lust-rious underground movie set Andy Warhol Gregory Markopolis Taylor Meade Superstars. Genius the lot, but at the moment not harmful to an industry that has made films and art with great character and direction, and money. As Cocteau said, "Even in disorder, there is order." I like their films, but I like all films. Warhol behaves like a man who has never seen a camera or movie. He behaves like the inventor, Tom Edison. He sets people in front of a stationary camera and asks them to stare blankly into the lens, or the Empire State Building appears and disappears. Warhol doesn't edit. He merely connects white leader together, which explains the appearing and disappearing, exposed under or underexposed, the total movie is eight hours. The underexposed part, one light-setting for the whole movie, is only three of those hours.

What ever happened to Baby Jane?

It jumped up her petticoat and bit her on her

Cocktail   Gingerale   Five Cents A Glass

Everyone can talk, drink, smoke, buy art, discuss 1930's musicals, and how movies, with the exception of those, haven't been good since the advent of sound, nothing good after Busby Berkley's at Warner Bros. in the Thirties.

"The second reel of Berkley's—oh, what's the name of that film? Just the second reel. Oh, you know the one—it was one of those Thirties' films—the one with the Piano Scene—great big piano keys and they all danced all over it. What a great scene! What the hell's the name of that movie?"

Out of a dark corner I hear:

"Where does Marlon come off making a million dollars a picture, and what is he doing with it?"

"Well. I'll have a drink. That should make me think of the name of that damn movie!"

"Dames!"

"What?"

"DAMES! That's the name of the movie!"

"Hell, you knew it all the time, you crazy galoot."

"Hey! Look at Andy's movie! It's getting close to where that light switches on, on top of the Empire State!"

It sure is, but not *that* way! What we need are good old American—and that's not to be confused with European—Art Films. But who delivers? Where do we find them? How much does it cost? Where do they get a quarter of a million dollars? What would they have to be to do it? Where do we go? It all depends on X Y Z, and no one seems to know the answer.

(But when the time comes, they'll appear.) America's where it can be done. Maybe the Europeans have a great start, because of government help. God forbid that happens here before the wealthy support the film! We all admire the Church for having given Michelangelo money to build his lasting work. But Greco and Goya and a lot of people were supported by patrons. Yes, I think that's the word. Patrons. Where are the Patrons? Patrons, if found and cornered, ask: "Why not get it from the Industry?"

It's a second- and third-generation industry. It's an industry.

Film is an art-form, an expensive art-form, it's the Sistine Chapel of the Twentieth Century, it's the best way to reach

10

people. The artist, not the industry, must take the responsibility for the entire work. Michelangelo did less than one quarter of the Sistine Chapel; yet directed all work, stone by stone, mural by mural, on and on and on.

Patrons. Patrons. That's the word.

But where are the angels? Even the flesh? Better still, WHERE'S THE CASH?

But even better still, WHERE ARE THE PEOPLE TO GIVE THE CASH TO??? Not to worry. No, not to worry. They'll be here when it's their turn to change the balance of power in the good old American Way; then my generation will have its say. Our grandfathers and fathers made it what it is today, they invented it. Can we sustain it? Because we've lost it. Can we fill the movie-gap? And take back our invention? And surpass the Europeans? Yes, when that Individual comes to town. Remember him? The Individual? Well, then, when it's his turn. Yes, we'd better do it then. Or I'm going to die a very cranky Individual, and I won't be alone. It's time for a transition shot.

INTERMISSION

September, 1969

The angels did appear—Peter Fonda, Bert Schneider, Bob Rafelson, Jack Nicholson, Bill Hayward, Terry Southern, Bobby Walker, Henry Jaglom, Paul Lewis, Leslie Kovacs and many others associated with Easy Rider.

Will Easy Do It
for Dennis Hopper

Dennis Hopper? Oh, yes, the intense, forthright, pale-eyed boy in *Rebel Without a Cause* and *Giant* and those ponderous late-fifties television dramas. What ever happened to Dennis Hopper?

What happened was that Hopper told Hollywood where to put its antediluvian system, was industry-blackballed, ate peyote, smoked pot, dressed like Billy the Kid, let his milk-chocolate hair grow untended, met Peter Fonda, dropped acid with him off-screen and on (*The Trip*), kept insisting that he could direct a significant film, proved he was right with *Easy Rider,* a moving account of young misfits crossing the Southwest on motorcycles (he wrote it with Fonda and Terry Southern, and co-starred, but directed it by himself, and promptly won the 1969 Cannes Festival award for the best movie by a new director), and came to New York to promote its local premiere.

And now he sits in a midtown actors' bar, empty this afternoon, except for a few aging chorus boys who have trailed in, dragging their airlines bags, for a beer between auditions. Some of them glance at him curiously. For one thing, he is wearing his felt outlaw's hat, Mexican shirt and Navaho talismans. For another, he is younger than almost anyone in the room. Actually, he is 33, but there is something distinctly untainted about him, something untouched, dedicated, committed. He is, in fact, utterly committed to moviemaking. This year, he dissolved his 1961 marriage to Brooke Heyward, Leland Heyward's daughter, because "the day I started *Easy Rider,* Brooke said, 'You are going after fool's gold,' and that didn't read too

by TOM BURKE

12

well with me. Brooke is groovy, we even have a beautiful little girl, but you don't say that to me, man, about something I've waited 15 years—no, all my life—to do."

He laughs his quick, oddly apologetic laugh, doodles invisibly with his finger on the side of his Irish coffee glass, says that he had thought all interviewers were old and square ("It's not what they ask, man, it's who they *are*"), and that he hadn't expected somebody young. "It's groovy, man. Beautiful. I feel very comfortable." For this reason, perhaps, he does not wait for questions. Instead, he says, "Dodge City. I come from Dodge City, Kansas. In movies about Dodge City, they always put in big mountains but there aren't any. Just endless wheat fields, this fantastic flat horizon line, incredible electric storms, sunsets like the northern lights. Every Saturday, I'd walk from the farm into town with my grandmother, who had her apron full of fresh eggs. We'd sell them and use the money to see whatever picture was playing: Roy Rogers, Gene Autry, Smiley Burnette. Then all the next week, I'd live that picture. If it was a war picture, I'd dig foxholes; if it was sword-fighting, I'd poke the cows with a stick. Those dark little Kansas theaters, Saturday afternoons, man, that was big news to me. The old cliché, dig? Like Thomas Wolfe wanting to see where the trains were going to. I wanted to see where those movies were coming from."

Eventually he saw. When he was 14, the family moved to San Diego. "I'm creative, man," he says, straight-faced, eyes smiling, "because of my big disappointment: seeing real mountains and real ocean for the first time. Wow, what a bringdown! The mountains in my head were much bigger than the Rockies. The Pacific was the horizon line in my wheat field. Anyway, I was terrible in school, because I didn't like reading. I've read maybe eight novels in my life. I'd rather live it, man, get out in the street, get it *on*. But I did win debating contests, and apprenticed, summers, at the La Jolla Playhouse, and did Shakespeare at the Old Globe Theater. When I went to Hollywood, though, I was going to be either a matador, a race-car driver or a boxer. In Spain, if you're broke and lousy in school, you become a matador. In Italy, you race cars. Here, you box, or act. I boxed and got beat up, so acting was the only thing left."

The bar's jukebox vibrates as The Fifth Dimension segues from "Aquarius" to "Let the Sunshine In." He smiles toward the music, gently asks the tired waiter for another drink, and recites the would-be movie actor's litany: impenetrable studios,

13

disinterested agents, starvation ("I stole milk from porches, occasionally I'd hit an orange juice"), a tiny television role, a big one, and sudden offers from five movie companies. "Columbia called first, and I was brought into Harry Cohn's huge office, with about a hundred Oscars stacked behind his desk in an arc, like a rainbow. I'd never seen an Oscar before." Laughing, he mimics the legendary Cohn. " 'I seen your TV show, kid, you got *it,* you're a natural, like Monty Clift! What else you done?' I told him about the Shakespeare, and he yelled to an assistant, 'Give this kid some numbers'—money—'and put him under contract! But we'll have to send him to a coach for a year, to take that Shakespeare out of him.' At that point, I said to Harry Cohn, 'Go —— yourself.' Whereupon I was barred from Columbia. I didn't go back there for 15 years, until they agreed to release *Easy Rider,* and I walked through those gates to start the editing. Freaky."

At Warners, things were happier, partly because he never had to talk to Jack Warner, mostly because of the two pictures he made with James Dean—*Rebel Without a Cause,* in 1955, and *Giant,* in 1956. "There'll never be anybody like Jimmy again, man. It was, in a strange way, a closer friendship than most people have, but it wasn't the kind of thing where he said, 'Let's go out and tear up the town.' Sometimes we'd have dinner. Also, we were into peyote and grass before anybody else. This is my 17th grass-smoking year. Sure, print it, why not? You can also say that that was real pot we smoked in *Easy Rider.* I've already been busted once for possession, in L.A., but that's another story.

"Anyway, about Jimmy: what we really had was a student-teacher relationship, the only one he ever had, as far as I know. When we were making *Rebel,* I just grabbed him one day and said, 'Look, man, I gotta know how you act, because you're the greatest!' So he asked me, very quietly, why I acted, and I told him what a nightmare my home life had been, everybody neurotic because they weren't doing what they wanted to do, and yelling at me when I wanted to be creative, because creative people ended up in bars." He looks around solemnly. "Which I later found out to be true. Anyway, Jimmy and I found we'd had the same experience at home, and that we were both neurotic and had to justify our neuroses by creating, getting the pain out and sharing it. He started watching my takes after that. I wouldn't even know he was there. Two days later, he'd come up and mumble, 'Why don't you try the scene *this* way.' And he was always right. His death blew my mind. I

14

couldn't get it together, man, for a long time afterward. Because I really believed in predestination—that something protected gifted people until they could realize their potential. Jimmy was going to direct, and he would have been great. What's wrong with most movie directors is that they understand one aspect of a film, like photography, editing, or acting, but not all the aspects together. Jimmy did. He'd started to refuse to take direction, because all he got was *bad* direction . . ."

After Dean's death, Dennis started refusing direction, too, from Henry Hathaway, among others. He and Hathaway clashed while making *From Hell to Texas* in 1958, and it got around that he was unemployable. Years passed before Hathaway rehired him, for a small role in *True Grit*, but Dennis doesn't regret the lean period. "I had to live out that rebellion," he asserts, his pace quickening as it always does when he speaks with conviction, "or I wouldn't have learned. If you don't refuse, at one point, to do what you don't believe in, you're never gonna grow, or get bigger than the guy who's telling you wrong. I got stronger. This time, when Henry started shooting, and said, 'No trouble from you, kid, this is a Big Duke picture, and Big Duke don't understand that Method ————,' I just nodded. I knew I was now technically proficient enough, and personally strong enough, to do Henry's number, and also do mine. There are advantages in working for the big studios once in a while. Like bread, for one. I consider it the same as, say, working for the Catholic Church in the Renaissance. If you want to paint the big ceiling, man, you gotta deal."

But for *Easy Rider,* no deals. When Dennis and Peter Fonda acted together in *The Trip* in 1967, they ended up going out into the desert and shooting the acid-trip sequences by themselves, with their own funds, because no one else, including director Roger Corman, wanted to take the time or spend the money. Dennis directed, and though he had been a professional photographer for some time, this was his first attempt at moviemaking. He was instantly hooked, but no one was willing to back Hopper and Fonda in their own venture. They both got involved in other people's motorcycle pictures: Peter's *The Wild Angels* made millions, and Dennis's *The Glory Stompers* at least showed a profit, "and Peter and I decided the only way we'd get backing was another bike film. But a *different* one.

Then Peter called me at, like 3 A.M., and said he'd been sitting around getting stoned and playing his guitar and he'd had this idea. It was *Easy Rider*. Our real luck came when Bert Schneider and Bob Rafelson said they'd produce it. They gave us complete control. They just said, 'Go and do your thing and come back and show us.' And we did, man. Except for the Mardi Gras scenes, we just started out on our bikes across the West and shot entirely in sequence, as things happened to us."

Then a scenario wasn't used? Wrong; a script was carefully completed before shooting, "but it was left flexible enough that we could add to it or change it as we traveled. Some things never changed. For instance, I knew that I wanted to use songs that were already popular, rather than a new score. I knew that Peter and I and the girls we meet would never be seen totally nude in the nude swimming scene, because I wanted to show the over-40 crowd that it is possible to play like innocent children in the nude without getting into sex. Even simple nudity would have killed the point.

"And I wanted to use actual residents of the towns we went into, and let them say pretty much what they would actually say when they saw our long hair and so on. I'd outline what I wanted in a scene, give them a few specific lines, and let them improvise from there. As for our characters, Peter's and mine, they were thoroughly set in advance. I've never seen a movie in which the director acted that he didn't come out the star, and it was important to me that Peter be the star, not because he's Peter Fonda, but because his character in the movie, Captain America, is the leader, the good guy. You can't have a John Wayne without a Ward Bond, though, so I took upon my character all the burden of explanation, the cynicism. Together, we're symbols of this country today—Captain America, man, is *today's* leader—and when the small-town lawyer joins up with us, you have a real American cross-section. As we watch them, we think of them as nice kids, but they're actually in their early thirties, an age when the Establishment says they should be working, contributing. Instead, they're peddling dope. Because that seems no worse to them than the Wall Street tycoon spending 80 per cent of his time cheating the government.

"Everybody seems confused about the end of the picture, and all I'm saying there is that we aren't very different from the two guys in the truck who shoot us. That all of us, man, are herd-instincted animals, that we all need each other. And *why* can't the different herds mingle? I was in the freedom march, man, Selma to Montgomery, and there was this guy at the side of the road who was urinating on us as we passed, and yelling 'White trash,' and I thought, 'Wow! Can't he see, can't he get it together? We only look different, we're all part of the same herd. He kept shouting at me, 'Hippy, Commie, long-hair!' Wow. I mean, *I* don't care if *he* has *short* hair!"

Guru hair vs. crewcuts, beads vs. golf shirts, motorcycles vs. Toyota Coronas; in rural America, the dichotomy proved more appalling than Dennis and Peter had dreamed. "Every restaurant, man, every roadhouse we went in, there was a Marine sergeant, or a football coach who started with, 'Look at the Commies, the queers, is it a boy or a girl?' We expected that. But the stories we heard along the way, man, true stories, of kids getting their heads broken with clubs or slashed with rusty razor blades—*rusty* blades, man—just because they passed through towns with long hair. And not just in the South. In Montrose, Colorado, where we made *True Grit,* I walked into a bar and immediately a guy swung at me, screaming, 'Get outta here, my son's in Vietnam,' and the local sheriff was right behind him, screaming that *his* son was in Vietnam, and I said, 'Now wait a minute,' that I was an actor and there with the movie, whereupon the boys' high school counselor started screaming to get out, that *his* son was in Vietnam. And I thought, 'What if I wasn't an actor, what if I was just traveling through and was thirsty?' So I said, 'Okay, I'm hitchhiking to the peace march,' whereupon eight guys jumped me. Incredible, but true, I swear.

"With *Easy Rider,* in Baton Rouge, the Vanilla Fudge was playing next door to our hotel, and when we went over, these beautiful local kids came up and said, 'Oh, wow, your hair's so long, man, we want to grow our hair like that.' They were so groovy. And in the hotel dining room, there's this table of senators, and one of them is screaming that Rockefeller is going to put a nigger in Bobby Kennedy's position—this was like three days after the assassination—and that if he does, they'll take care of the nigger, because they know how to deal, down here, with niggers in politics. At that point, *I* told *him* to get out. But, man, how do you get it together? Those beautiful kids next door, full of love, grooving on the Vanilla Fudge, and that guy? At what point do *they* turn into *him*? Maybe he was once a groovy kid too . . ."

He shakes his head. As if on cue, the Fifth Dimension sings again. He smiles a moment at the irony, then says, "I dunno, it's a nightmare. What I want to say with *Easy Rider* is, 'Don't

17

be scared, go and try to change America, but if you're gonna wear a badge, whether it's long hair or black skin, learn to protect yourselves. Go in groups, but go. When people understand that they can't tromp you down, maybe they'll start accepting you. Accepting *all* the herds.' "

It is time for him to go, and we start out of the bar, but he does not seem to want to stop talking, about films, the one he has made, the ones he's going to make. In the process of his divorce settlement, he explains, he relinquished to his wife the house, the car, his motorcycle, and his art collection—he had bought Warhol, Rauschenberg and Jasper Johns when Robert Scull was still collecting taxis—so that he would be allowed to keep his share of the *Easy Rider* profits, whatever they may be. "I took a chance, man, but I believe in the picture, and it's going to give me my freedom—to make more like it, and to get out of cities. I've noticed that a film I'm directing is affected by the place I'm making it in, and in cities, I get sick. You don't have to sit in the L.A. smog the whole year to make a movie. I've got to get back to the country, to an earth feeling, like when I was a kid. You know: touch a leaf, see if it has bugs under it." He laughs. "I've gotta see if I really am this sensitive loner, or if that's just an image I made up for myself."

Outside, the daylight turns the Simonized surface of his hired limousine to silver, and he shields his eyes. "Taos, man," he says, getting in. "Taos, New Mexico. There's freedom there. They don't mind long hair. The herds mingle."

As the car edges into Eighth Avenue, he glances out once at the filthy street, then closes his eyes, preferring his vision of Taos.

Jack Nicholson — Talking and Talked about

He's the most talked about actor of the year. Like Dustin Hoffman, Jack Nicholson of *Easy Rider* at the Charles Cinema has suddenly become motion picture news. Only he is newer than Hoffman of *The Graduate* and *Midnight Cowboy*.

Nicholson doesn't compare himself to Hoffman, whom he much admires as the finest new talent of cinema, but to the late Humphrey Bogart.

"Like Bogart I am essentially a character actor," said the affable, bearded, long-haired young man, who appears to be in his early thirties, but under that beard could be any age.

"Bogie made 20 to 30 appearances on Broadway and in pictures before *Petrified Forest* attracted attention to him and made him a star. I've worked in several films as writer, producer and actor before *Easy Rider,* but it wasn't until now that the magazine writers started to interview me.

"When you are a character actor you are never so well known as when you get to be a star and are assigned to one similar role after another. Clark Gable always took a part with which the public identified him. There was never any surprise and possible disappointment as a result."

Jack Nicholson, I now venture to prophesy, will become famous with the film-going public for one particular gesture in *Easy Rider*. To his own amazement, he knows that it is highly probable. Already it is the fashion in Hollywood among the "in" group to flap their arms like an aroused pelican's wings and utter a wierd sound of ni-ck, ni-ck" when taking the first drink of the day, or of the occasion.

It comes from Nicholson's characterization, and while he

by MARJORY ADAMS

asked me not to reveal the combination of vulgarities which the "ni-ck" represents he said it all started with an expression of an old barfly called Gypsy Bill. It is something like starting a drink with the expressionistic "Vroom."

But so colorful is the gesture that Nicholson already knows its power of attraction. The 5-year-old daughter of Dennis Hopper, director and co-star of *Easy Rider*, followed Jack around begging "Do Nick-nick."

When I, too, requested a private showing Jack looked at me in disapproval.

"I am not going to make this into a parlor stunt," said he sternly.

He tried to divert my attention by describing his outfit, which he had worn on the plane from Philadelphia.

There was the Air Force bush jacket, the Navy work pants with the bell bottoms taken out and the T-shirt bearing on its front the words, "Property of the U.S.C. Athletic Department," which he had bought in New Jersey at a second hand shop.

But he was most proud of the "spectator shoes," a concoction of elaborate eyelet-worked brown leather and spectacular white kid which Nicholson believes to be the only such shoes now extant.

"They are just like the ones my father used to wear in the early 1930's in the Easter Parade," he said. "I've been looking for some since I went to Hollywood and finally managed to get them in a Hollywood wardrobe department."

Asked if he was already recognized on the street, Nicholson said *Easy Rider* is beginning to get him public attention. Previously people would look at him vaguely and figure they had seen him somewhere.

They indeed had seen him—he was "Poet" in the popular, if not artistic, success, *Hell's Angels on Wheels*. As soon as he had finished the picture he was off the set, and no one in the studio ever bothered to get in touch with him again or arranged for any publicity with his being in it.

"Many people must have seen it because it grossed $6,000,000 and is continuing to grow," commented Nicholson. "But my name has never been connected with it in the mind of the public."

Even when he played Weary Riley in *Studs Lonigan*, which was the first picture Haskell Wexler photographed (although he was billed as associate producer) the name of Jack Nicholson never came up in the publicity campaign.

His latest film outside *Easy Rider* is Vincente Minnelli's *On a Clear Day* with Barbra Streisand. Nicholson isn't happy because Minnelli wouldn't let him wear his cherished brown and white spectator shoes.

"What happens regarding your beard?" I asked. "Don't you have to shave it off occasionally?"

"I don't cut it until it interferes with my breathing or unless the director demands it," he answered.

"Barbers bug me. That is, hair-cuts do. When the barber asks, 'How's that?' as he hands you a mirror, you are supposed to answer, 'That looks fine.'

"But what I want to do is get out into the air and let the blood rush back to my face."

Nicholson prefers different types of roles and speaks with affection of *The Raven* in which he played a milk-toast kind of young man. What pleased him was being with Vincent Price, Peter Lorre and Boris Karloff. That was Big League stuff. Naturally his name was not included in studio publicity with these top-notchers.

"I was co-producer and co-author of *Head* in which the Monkees starred," volunteered the actor helpfully.

"Sorry, I didn't see it," I replied.

"You are among the great majority," sighed Nicholson.

Many of Nicholson's films are better known in Europe than here. He was co-producer, writer and co-star with Millie Perkins in *Ride in the Whirlwind,* for instance. Another of his Westerns is *The Shooting,* also with Miss Perkins.

They ran for 15 weeks in Paris—but in this country people don't seem to have heard of them, he volunteered.

Nicholson wrote the scenario for *The Trip* and says of LSD that he can take it or leave it alone. It is a lot less compulsive a habit than liquor, he maintains. What he can't understand is why people who booze a lot think LSD so immoral a habit.

"If I don't complain about them and their liquor why do they complain about my associates when they go on a trip?" he chides.

Easy Rider's *Soundtrack*

In the second scene of the Peter Fonda-Dennis Hopper film *Easy Rider* there is a cameo part for Phil Spector. The scene takes place at a small airport and involves a silent transaction in which Spector buys an enormous quantity of dope from our two cycling heroes—some white powder that can be sniffed, probably cocaine. Spector, looking freaky as ever in a huge Rolls—one reviewer commented that he looked very gangster-ish—ducks every time a plane takes off. Then he tests the merchandise and seems to relax. Apparently, his ears have taken over: the roar of the engines, which has always been present, suddenly seems oppressively loud, filling the theater and, incredibly, even the screen, dominating the visuals in a Phil Spector apotheosis, an almost literal wall of sound. Spector looks safe as milk. Cut to Fonda and Hopper on their motorcycles, winding away from the scene of their financial triumph as a familiar guitar line comes over the soundtrack. Soon, John Kay of Steppenwolf is singing "The Pusher."

Fonda and Hopper are rock fans and they are friendly with rock musicians. But neither could be described as a music head —Hopper, who took most of the responsibility for the music, doesn't even collect records—and that is interesting, because *Easy Rider* is the only film I know that not only uses rock well —though that is rare enough—but also does justice to its spirit. Clearly, the spirit of rock—and now I am talking about the American variant; that the English usually refer to it as "pop" is significant in this context—is not so much the culmination of a form as of a subculture. It would be difficult if not impossible to understand this subculture without intelligent reference

by ROBERT CHRISTGAU

to the music. In fact, *Easy Rider* is a double rarity—not only does it use rock successfully, it also treats the youth-dropout thing successfully. You can't have one without the other.

So few movies use rock correctly because the people that make movies, who are even more avaricious and ignorant than the people who sell records, lust after the extra profits of a soundtrack album, which means commissioning one composer, or group, to do a mostly instrumental score. Rock composers don't work well on order and aren't good at background music —when they try (John Sebastian on *You're a Big Boy Now* or Harry Nilsson on *Skidoo!*) their results are even more insipid than those of the pros. (Booker T. Jones was able to write a superb score for *Uptight!* because the M. G.s are not a vocal group—though Booker's vocal debut in the film was auspicious —and because his experience in the Stax studios prepared him for such an effort.) The results have been somewhat better in theme songs (Roger McGuinn's "Child of the Universe," Paul Simon's "Mrs. Robinson") but even in that area the same strictures apply: songs-to-order are a drag. Thus far, I know of only two cases in which a rock composer has hired out to do an even passable score. Both were English and both, properly, used at least half a dozen songs and a minimum of la-dee-dah: Mike Hugg (of Manfred Mann) on *Up the Junction,* and Spencer Davis and Stevie Winwood on *Here We Go Round the Mulberry Bush.* The music for *Wild in the Streets,* by Barry Mann and Cynthia Weil, both music industry pros rather than inspired amateurs, was also pretty good, but the performances (remember Max Frost?) were lousy. (It was better than *Privilege,* though.)

Movies can use rock in other ways, of course. There have been a number of good music movies—the Beatle flicks and *Monterey Pop* (which has a much superior rock and roll predecessor, *The TAMI Show,* released in 1965 and starring—get ready—the Beach Boys, Marvin Gaye, Smokey Robinson, Chuck Berry, James Brown, and the Rolling Stones; it was shot black-and-white on videotape and has either disappeared or disintegrated; if the former, someone should find it and exhibit it). Some underground film-makers have used rock well without paying for it (no profits, no lawsuit): the Everly Brothers can be heard in the background of Andy Warhol's *Poor Little Rich Girl,* and Warren Sonbert has juxtaposed the naive formalism of the various girl groups to his own young-jaded formlessness. Antonioni in *Blow-Up* and Lester in *Petulia* have misused rock to epitomize some vague aspect of our

Decaying Culture, but at least they had the taste to choose good rock (the Yardbirds, Big Brother, the Grateful Dead). But in Peter Bogdanovich's *Targets,* a scrupulously realistic movie which involves considerable driving around the freeways in a Mustang with the radio blaring, the radio station apparently programs directly off an 87-cent dance party record picked up at a Rexall.

The reason Bogdanovich couldn't have real music is that his budget is small and re-use rates tend to be prohibitive. Yet I wonder. Bogdanovich is a hip young guy, not some displaced brassiere manufacturer, and his movie was honest and interesting. I feel certain he could have screened the movie for enough groups to find a few who were willing to give him a break. On a higher level—he used songs by Steppenwolf, the Band, the Byrds, Jimi Hendrix, and the Electric Flag, and he needed specific songs, not just snatches of background noise—that was Hopper's method, and only the Band soaked him a little (in their warm Woodstock way, of course). He took the trouble because he knew it was worth the trouble. (He didn't take the trouble with billboards, which also can't be reproduced without permission, and the film is doubtless worse for it; I am a billboard freak as well as a music freak.) He resisted pressure to commission a soundtrack because he understood the profound emotional value of known songs. He knew he could not make his movie honestly without real music.

In many respects, *Easy Rider* is similar to *Nothing But a Man,* which contracted its music from Motown. Both films are low-budget treatments of oppressed subcultures that rely on music for cohesion and spiritual succor. In both films, the music references are somewhat literary: in *Nothing But a Man* there is a mock fistfight during Mary Wells' "You Beat Me to a Punch," and in *Easy Rider* "Born to Be Wild" plays as the heroes hit the road. That's okay even if it is romantic and unsophisticated. The music is romantic and unsophisticated, too, finally, and it would take a convolutionist who would make Warren Sonbert look like Sam Goldwyn to deal with the Byrds in as carefully distanced a way as Sonbert has dealt with the Supremes.

It's also okay because the message of the movie—like the message of the music—is itself romantic and unsophisticated. American rock has always had a love-hate thing with technology (its message is so often pastoral, but its medium is intractably electric) and with America itself (the message once again negative and the form positive). *Easy Rider,* with its central image of two longhairs on gleaming chrome motor-cycles, one decorated with stars and stripes, following the road through an otherwise unspoiled American West of buttes and deserts and benevolent patches of green, embodies the same dichotomy with reference to the same subculture. It has the same youthful romanticism, too, glorifying the outcasts and detesting and fearing the straights. You could even say that its dark side was anticipated spiritually by all those teen death songs that don't seem quite so funny after all. Think about it: isn't Tom Hayden the leader of the pack?

Rolling Stone *Raps with* Peter Fonda

"When I did *Tammy and the Schmuckface,* I got a lot of fan mail. Thousands of letters a week, asking me for my autograph and my picture. When I did the *Wild Angels,* I didn't get much fan mail. When I did *The Trip,* and now that I've done *Easy Rider,* I get letters from people saying, 'What do I do?' 'How do I talk to my father?' 'How do I stop trying to kill myself? How do I learn something, how can I live?' Nobody's asking me for my picture and my autograph anymore. So the movie I'm making means nothing. The life I'm making obviously means something to these people."

*   *   *

In his 29 years, Peter Fonda has acted in a lot of bad movies, been busted for grass, been blasted by the press for being plastic and by his relatives for being outrageous. All that's over now, since *Easy Rider.* He recalls stopping his car during the cross-country filming and looking back at all the trucks and cars and camera equipment and people getting out and waving traffic on, and thinking, "Far out! That's all my company. That's all there because I wanted to ride a motorcycle and I needed money to build it."

"It's the wrong way to go about it. . . . I was taking pleasure in it rather than enjoying it. When I was just doing it, I had a better time. But there were moments when I did stop and look back and reflect. I'd say, 'Jesus. That's my company! But I'm supposed to be a failure'!"

Fonda had not only been telling himself that, it was what he'd been told. "Weren't you ever told that? Or did you kill

by *ELIZABETH CAMPBELL*

your parents when you were young?" "You're not what we wanted," Fonda remembers, was the message passed down the dining room table. "That goes for me, and everybody I know, and everybody I don't know and their parents and their police, and their government and their church. . . ."

In the old days, before he discovered cannabis, Fonda carried a loaded gun. And he was a crack shot. "Then I met this chick in New York, and she saw a strung out, paranoid Pisces. And she said, 'Here. Smoke a little of this instead.' And I did. And I got ripped. And I stopped wearing a gun. And I stopped drinking, and I got less and less violent."

Yet he does not consider himself a pacifist. "I know one thing, though. If I pull a carrot out of the ground, I'm going to eat it. I won't throw it back on the ground and let it rot. If I cut a tree down, I'm going to put it to use. Those are both living, breathing organisms. And if I pull a gun, I'm going to put it to use."

That, says Fonda, is a big change for somebody who was programmed to be a Boy Scout. "That's what my old man wanted me to be. He was an Eagle Scout. Eagle Scouts became chiefs of staff, or big generals. Somebody who goes that far into order and system is almost a fascist. And my father's a *liberal*."

One of the biggest influences on Fonda has been the Indian philosopher, Krishnamurti, who insists that people ask themselves—and not him—the questions. Fonda met Krishnamurti accidentally on the beach one day, and to him it was like meeting Jesus. He talked to him for hours, about many things. One of them was smoking grass.

"He looked at me and said, 'I don't smoke grass.' And I said, 'That's true. But you have your monogram on your shirt, and you comb your hair in a way that pleases you. And you probably drink coffee, or tea.' He said, 'I drink tea.' I said, 'I smoke grass.' "

Fonda and his co-star Dennis Hopper actually turn on in the film, but that, he said, isn't a measure of the film's truth and honesty. "It's just a publicity gig, to talk about it. We just turned on because that's the way we wanted to do it. It was also fun."

Fonda considers *Easy Rider* "*cinéma vérité* in allegory terms."

The film is really a lecture-demonstration on the conclusions Peter Fonda has come to regarding the United States of America in 1969. It has been very successful in the box office, and almost as fortunate with the critics. Most of them praise the film's integrity and its portrayal of American hypocrisy and discrimination, but many complained about Fonda and Hopper. "We couldn't identify with them," they said.

Perhaps their protests are directed towards a certain feeling of betrayal; "If these guys represent the younger generation, why won't they let us understand them?"

The basic assumption is that the characters played by Fonda and Hopper *are* Fonda and Hopper, or at least speak for them. The irony of it all is that the lesson as prescribed by Fonda is understood exactly the way he intended it to be understood. Critics come away saying, "Those guys aren't free! they aren't even very happy." Fonda says they weren't supposed to be:

"I play a character called Captain America. I'm Peter Fonda, I'm *not* Captain America, so I'm playing somebody else. I am representing everybody who feels that freedom can be bought, who feels that you can find freedom through other things, like riding motorcycles through the air or smoking grass. In this country, we've all been programmed to retire. We get our thing together, no matter who goes down.

"My movie is about the *lack* of freedom, not about freedom. My heroes are not right, they're wrong. The only thing I can end up doing is killing my character. I end up committing suicide; that's what I'm saying that America is doing. People do go in and they think. 'Look at those terrible rednecks, they killed those two free souls, who needed to love, blah, blah, blah.' That's something we have to put up with.

"We don't give out any information through dialogue. We have a very loose plot, nothing you can follow. You can't predict what's going to happen, and that puts everybody off. People want it predicted for them, they want violence to happen when they expect it to happen, so they can deal with it, they want sex to be a certain way and drugs to be a certain way and death to be a certain way. And it ain't. Neither is freedom. 'Easy Rider' is a Southern term for a whore's old man, not a pimp, but the dude who lives with a chick. Because he's got the easy ride. Well, that's what's happened to America, man. Liberty's become a whore, and we're all taking an easy ride."

Easy Rider was produced by Fonda, directed by Dennis Hopper, and written by them with Terry Southern. Fonda says that the film is exactly the way they wanted it, with one exception. They had wanted to use "It's Alright, Ma," for the ending. Dylan saw the film, as did the other artists whose music Fonda and Hopper wanted to use. The idea was to have the music which accompanies the cross-country cycling scenes reflect current times. All the groups approved the film, and okayed the use of their music. The Band walked out after the performance without saying anything, then called Fonda at 3 A.M. to say that their song ("The Weight") was the only good one in the film, and could they write all the music? They were persuaded there wasn't enough time.

"If there are mistakes in the film, they're my mistakes and Dennis' mistakes. Nobody foisted anything on us—it's exactly the way we wanted it, with the exception of Mr. Zimmerman.

"I give no hope to the audience at the end of the film, and Mr. Zimmerman says, That's wrong, you've got to give them hope!

"I said, OK, Bob, what do you have in mind?

"He said, 'Well, re-shoot the ending, and have Fonda run his bike into the truck and blow up the truck.'

"Dennis said, 'No, give me your song, Bob.'

"He said, 'How about you don't use the song and we make another movie.'

"Dennis said, 'No, no, how about we don't make another movie and we use the song.'

"He said, 'The song's pretentious.'

"I said, 'He not busy being born is busy dying.'

"He said, 'Never mind that, man, have you heard my new album? It's a whole new number. We've got to give them *love*.'

"I said, 'I understand that. You have to love them, but you cannot give them love.'

"I kept thinking, Dylan sounds right. A lot of people are saying, 'Fonda, Dylan's right. You can't give them hopeless negative vibes.' I thought, you can't give them love either. Krishnamurti pointed that out. You can't give them a thing. They've got to take it, otherwise there's nothing happening. Freedom can't be second hand information.

"Dylan's one of my biggies. I'm my only hero, but he's one of my biggies. Him and John Lennon. I can't understand how he can say how he made 'It's Alright, Ma' to fill out the side of an album.

"So he feels embarrassed about protesting. The truth of the matter is 'He not busy being born is busy dying.' That's the truth of the matter. [He quotes the verse from "It's Alright, Ma" which begins "A question in your nerves is lit."]

"That was the end of our movie. He made us take that off

29

the end of the movie. He looked at it, and all he could hear was his bad voice and his lousy harmonica. His bad voice! . . . Oh, my god! . . . His lousy harmonica! I don't understand that. Come on, get it straight, Mr. Zimmerman!

"My name's Fonda, and it's been Fonda for years. And I won't renounce *Tammy and the Doctor.* I call it *Tammy and the Schmuckface,* because it's a bullshit movie, but it plays on the tube, and I don't try to buy the negative back and not have anybody see it.

"You can't forget the past, you can't effectively do a frontal lobotomy."

Fonda was questioned closely about other decisions made in the film when he was in San Francisco. The questions were those which might be asked of a friend who made a movie: "Why did you shoot the commune sequence that way?" "What kind of treatment did you get from the people you ran into?"

Answers: He thinks the commune sequence is the weakest in the movie; the line he wishes weren't there is "They're gonna make it," in the commune sequence, and they got a mixture of contempt for having long hair and interested admiration for making a Movie.

Whatever the reporters may have felt about Fonda and *Easy Rider* before talking with them, they left, without exception, liking him and thinking he was *real.*

For one thing, he looks like them. He wore blue jeans and a blue tee shirt and a suede jacket, which he designed himself and had made. (He wore the same outfit on the Joey Bishop show.) He wears a watch which tells all: even, with the aid of a sextant, where on earth he is. He carries about plans for a sailboat he wants to build. He has a neat beard, says it's because he doesn't like to shave, not because he wants to prove something.

He also had with him a horoscope, which a friend had done in exchange for a poem. His sun is in Pisces, in the tenth house, close to mid-heaven (A sign of success). His ascendent is Gemini. His moon is in Virgo, and it is in opposition to his Sun. Mercury in Pisces is also in opposition to Neptune in Virgo. Astrologically speaking, the opposition may be one explanation for his life and hard times.

After a mixed-up and geographically confusing childhood, Fonda was sent to an exclusive Eastern prep school. When he left in disgrace, his father sent him to live with his aunt and uncle in Omaha.

The Fonda family is socially prominent in Omaha—Henry

Fonda didn't have to leave home to become a struggling young actor—he could have stayed in Omaha and become a midwestern tycoon. Peter was instructed to stay in Omaha and finish college at the University of Omaha—no degree, no bread.

When Fonda walked into the studios of KMPX-FM in San Francisco last month, the program director, Tom Swift, greeted him lovingly, like an old friend.

"Man, you changed my life!"

Swift was a sophomore at the University of Omaha when an interview with Fonda appeared in the school newspaper. He recalls that Fonda expressed many of the things he had been thinking, and arranged to get to know him.

The two of them spent endless evenings drinking, knowing something was wrong but not knowing what it was, and trying to figure out how to·get out of Omaha. One night they put on eye patches, trench coats and berets in French Underground fashion and planted a fake bomb in the Omaha Greyhound bus station. They tipped off the police and watched. The caper was a sensation in the Omaha press.

Swift grew up in Omaha, and was perhaps as aware as one could be, without having gone anywhere else. But Fonda had been everywhere, and he exposed Swift to new influences, new ideas. "I had never met any artists or writers, and I mentioned that once," Swift recalls. "He said, 'That's not true. You're an artist, and you're a writer.'

"He got me to see myself as a whole bundle of possibilities."

During his early years at the University of Omaha, Fonda wanted to be a writer, and only later decided to become an actor. He tried out for plays put on at school—one of the first was *Picnic*, in which he played the rich kid and Tom Swift played the kid from the other side of the tracks. He graduated in three years, and set out for Broadway, and afterwards Hollywood. Swift says Fonda hasn't changed much since the Omaha days. "The only change is that he's done some of the things he said he'd do."

It was not easy to get the money to make *Easy Rider*. Fonda says he ultimately succeeded because he asked the right question at the right time. "I didn't ask for too much bread, and the way I laid it out, it embarrassed people into making the picture."

Fonda took no money for producing it or writing it; the money he had to be paid as a union actor he turned back to the company after deducting taxes. Dennis Hopper, broke at the time, was paid a minimal $150 a week. Now, it won't be long —*Easy Rider* is going to be fantastically financially successful.

And that, says Fonda, is the one real Hollywood requirement. "They reject me, until it makes money at the box office, then I'm their darling. But they still hold me in contempt on the one hand and in awe on the other. In contempt, because I've shown them a mirror of their own greed, and in awe, because I was able to do something they can't do, which was simply to make a motion picture honestly."

The options now open to those concerned in the success of *Easy Rider* are now almost limitless. Jack Nicholson, who is everybody's favorite in the movie, put it this way: "It's hard to make a movie. It really is hard to make a movie. So people who can actually do something are in tremendous demand."

After a success, Nicholson says, "Your problem is to keep from going insane over all the alternatives you have."

Nicholson, Hopper and Fonda are dealing with the problem of success in a somewhat less than traditional Hollywood fashion. Nicholson, who wrote *The Trip* and co-wrote *Head,* is going to direct a movie. He made that decision before the release of *Easy Rider.* "I had the ability to look at the part and say, 'Oh, people are gonna like that. I'm gonna get hot.' I've always known the movie was gonna be a big success. . . . I'd better set a couple of things, because though I've never been successful in the popular kind of way, I've seen it. And I know that I'm not the most constant person in the world . . . I like to change my mind a lot. So I wanted to set a couple of things before I got swept away."

Hopper has gone back to working on the first script he ever wrote; an interwoven western, called *The Last Movie.* And Fonda is still trying to do something he's wanted to do for some time—a film on the American Revolution. "People always say, the American Revolution, which one? I say, 'You mean you've separated yourself from the one that went down 200 years ago? You think it stopped? And we've gotten into something new? Well, it ain't new, and we haven't finished it, we haven't implemented the Bill of Rights.' "

He wants to take the film from the lowest point, Valley Forge. And this time, he says, "*Paths of Glory* is going to make money."

He has not as yet been successful in financing the film. But he is confident he will be. He says he keeps going back, always wanting the same thing, only now, "Each time I hit them I've made more money in the box office with *Easy Rider.*

"So now they're calling me and saying, 'Well, what do you want to do now?'

"I say, *'Conceived in Liberty.'* "

" 'Well, yeah, we've talked about that. Maybe if you get a package together.'

"I say, 'No, No, No. That's not right. That's not what you have to say. What you have to say is, GREAT! How much do you want? And then you have to say, GREAT! Of course you want to direct it, too, don't you? GREAT! Are you going to star in it? We'd like you to, if you will.' "

Even though nobody has had that conversation with him yet, Fonda says it will happen. "They'll give it to me, because they think that it's hip to give it to me, and that they'll make money with me, because I'm 'the hottest young actor in the business.' It's not true . . . I just happen . . . I grew up inside that industry, so I know what makes it tick."

Fonda and his wife and two children live in Beverly Hills. Their next door neighbor is Alfonso Bell, a conservative Republican congressman. Bell drives a Continental; Fonda drives a Volkswagen. "But I used to have Continentals. One time I had seven cars in my driveway. I couldn't decide which to drive in the morning . . . it's all gone. I don't have anything to say about that anymore, to anybody. I came back on 250 gammas and saw these seven cars sitting in my driveway, and they were rusting, and they were just machinery, grinding to a halt, right in front of my eyes."

He loves his VW. "It's purely anonymous, I don't get busted, it starts every time I start it and stops every time I stop it. (He did rent a Continental during the filming of *Easy Rider,* when he got tired of asking people for keys to dressing rooms. "I figured out what you do with a Continental—live in it!")

He doesn't take acid anymore, but feels he learned a lot from it. "Acid," Fonda says, "is to mental disorder what penicillin is to bacterial disorder." He had some bad trips, but says that "I was hip that the reason I was having bad acid trips was that I had a lot of hang-ups."

His wife's name is Susan, but he calls her "my old lady" or, more often, "my lady."

"She's gone through a lot of changes with me, and it certainly is difficult for her. I am a difficult person . . . I'm an evangelist. I move out when I work. I remove myself totally from everything. It must be freaky to be in love with somebody . . . she's in love with me . . . and see him just split, while he's sitting in the chair. But she understands it, and she copes with it. She knows that I love her. She knows it's not just a word. And she knows that I love my children.

"I have two children . . . I have two hostages to fortune. When I first heard that phrase from Jack Kennedy, I thought 'What does he mean, "He who has children gives hostages to fortune?" What's he trying to do, be Chairman Mao?' Well, then I had two kids. Hostages to fortune. I put away the gun."

Bridget, five, is an Aquarius, and Justin, three, is a Cancer. Fonda says that when his mind is "clear and quiet," Bridget can read his mind. He tells about times when she has known where he was taking her, before he told her . . . and when she knew he was supposed to do something, when he hadn't mentioned it. (Judging from a picture of her that he carries with him, she is capable of that and more.) He says getting married was "something we did for Them."

"We don't relate to it at all. There's danger lurking in that type of action . . . it's a false goal . . . it's false security. Marriage is bullshit. If you can't handle relationships without guidelines, if you need a book, if you need a code, if you need a vow, you ain't married, you don't even like your old lady."

Fonda believes that the moment a decision is made as to pain or pleasure, real enjoyment stops. "Suppose we're going swimming. The water's 78 degrees, great surf, perfect for body surfing, the air is about 85, and a light warm breeze, and we're on the beach, rolling around. We run in the water, and we're splashing around, and surfing in and swimming out, and I turn to you, and I say, 'God, isn't it a beautiful day!' It comes to a crashing halt. From that moment on the entire relationship is based on something from the past. It's a comparative day, it's a comparative reality, and it's not there."

Distortions enter relationships when decisions are made, Fonda believes. "Up to a point, nothing's happened that's insult or flattery. Somebody comes up to you and says, 'asdfghjkl.' And you heard, 'You're beautiful.' And you think, 'Far out, what a great dude he is.' Or you hear, 'asdfghjkl,' and you hear, 'You're a fool.' And you say, 'What an asshole he is, he doesn't even know me.' It's the same thing, insult or flattery, pain or pleasure. It's all interpretation of the mind based on one thing: fear."

Fonda believes, along with Krishnamurti, that abstract thought implies a kind of distortion. "I'm not separating myself from life anymore, from any part of it. I *am* the action, and it's not a question of wanting or not wanting. There's no hope or despair, there's no choice, even."

People have asked him if the presidential election wasn't a

case where he had to make a choice. "I said, 'There's *never* a choice, man, there's never a choice.' I would have voted for Bobby Kennedy. There was no choice.

"Nixon and Humphrey? No choice at all. I voted for Cleaver."

He thinks heroin, and in fact anything, is better than speed. He says he's tried to talk people out of shooting speed, but it doesn't work . . . they don't believe him, either. "They're exposed to a lie, and they assume that all things therefore have been lied about, and all things will be lied about. And there's no way you can convince them. You'd think that I would be one of the few people who could come up and say, 'Hey, man, don't do speed.' And the cat would say, 'He said it. King Drug said it.'

"But it doesn't work. Not when their mothers are taking amphetamines, and everybody's taking bennies to do an exam . . . of course it can't work."

He believes you can't tell people things. They have to be shown. "If I were to stand up like I'm talking to you now in the motion picture, and say, 'I'm dealing in fear, ladies and gentlemen, and fear is what's screwing you up, fear's fucking you right out of your seats,' they're gonna turn it off and put their fingers in their ears. They're gonna turn away and say, 'I didn't hear that, who is he to tell me that?' "

By keeping his mouth shut, he believes he can involve the audience on a much stronger level. And on that level, it is impossible to deny that *Easy Rider* is a success. Whatever people think of the movie, or of Fonda as an actor, they all walk out of the theater talking and arguing about where America is at, and where youth is at. And without even knowing that anybody wanted them to think about these things.

Fonda is sensitive to criticism; he knows that much of it is based on a misunderstanding of the goals of the movie, but the misunderstanding still hurts. "Those are *my* balls up there, on the screen."

But he says he refuses to give a performance. "The only performance I'm going to give is my life."

Introduction to
Easy Rider

Frederic Tuten teaches American literature at the City College of New York, is an art critic and contributing editor of Arts Magazine, *and writes about films for* Vogue.

Easy Rider: the return of the 'fifties *Wild Ones,* the son of the 'sixties *Wild Angels?* An exposé of the pot-smoking, acid-dropping, sex-crazed, cryptofascist bike maniacs? No. In *Easy Rider* the bikes are incidental, they might as well be horses; although there is an episode of a bad acid trip, pot is not exposed but promoted, treated as a soothing Indian peace pipe, formal and loving. The two riders in the film belong to no bike pack; Wyatt and Billy line up with the American pantheon of paired comrade heroes: Deerslayer and Chingachgook, Ishmael and Queequeg, Huck Finn and Jim, Sal Paradise and crazy Dean Moriarty of Kerouac's *On the Road*—all frontier lovers, territory-ahead travellers, innocent or doomed, or innocently doomed.

   Easy Rider is a conglomerate of so many basic impulses and myths in our culture that even while you move along with it, wonderingly, there is an abiding sense of a familiar terrain— the classic nineteenth-century American landscape, a violent pastoral, as if there existed simultaneously on one huge canvas the silence-drenched crags and lakes of Cole and Bierstadt, Remington's torrents of horses, Indians, dust, and cavalry or his scenes of cowboys at night campfires, and George Catlin's Indians hunting buffalo and placid wigwam encampments. *Easy Rider*'s heroic, brutal landscape is devoid of transcendental evil in man or nature. Its soil is not shadowed by Hawthornesque puritanical guilt; there are no gloomy paths into demonic forests. Even in moral darkness, America is a sunshine land.

by FREDERIC TUTEN

Much of the film's ebullience, voluptuous surface, reductive characterizations, its naivete, are in a sense in keeping with the image of this violent/pastoral America. *Easy Rider* has its origins in the fabric of the action-journey myth of our culture: Whitman's space-time flights in *Song of Myself,* Woody Guthrie's hobo-folk mystique in *Bound for Glory,* and Kerouac's frantic beat travelogue—all promising that the individual, the frontier, America, are still free. But Wyatt and Billy are the last of the open-road heroes: the road, the film suggests, is no longer open to a traffic of free-spirited riders.

"This used to be a helluva good country; I can't understand what's gone wrong with it," says the young Southern ACLU lawyer to the pair after the three have been hassled out of a Southern diner as "Yankee queers." What *is* going on is a cultural civil war. Implicit in the politics of *Easy Rider* are the Chicago Convention, the civil rights struggles, the Berkeley People's Park conflict, the California grape boycott, Viet-Nam. These are covert concerns expressed dialectically through the film's nostalgia for a still beautiful America and Americans: Indians dead and living, small ranchers, hippie communards, liberal dreamers, pot-smoking motorcycle saddle bums, Billy and Wyatt.

The morality of *Easy Rider* is as simplistic as a Western, except that its heroes are the outlaws, and its villains, the dangerously uptight, violent law-and-order Americans. This social paradigm is played out against a landscape, itself not merely a background, but a character. The Southwestern, Western, and Southern landscape Billy and Wyatt bike through seems a remnant of some spirit of an America that was, a presence so strong as to almost engulf the humans in the film. *Easy Rider* stretches into a time when Emerson and Thoreau believed in America's "crazies" and when the Indians were making their last sad stands.

The framework of *Easy Rider* is deceptively simple because it follows a traditional picaresque structure. Wyatt and Billy are paid off as middlemen in a cocaine deal on the Mexican border, Wyatt throws away his watch in a gesture of defiance of time and they head off, via the high desert roads, for New Orleans to celebrate Mardi Gras. Both long-haired and riding high-barred chromed motorcycles—Billy in his Kit Carson fringed jacket and bush hat, Wyatt in a stars and stripes helmet and black leather jacket with a miniature American flag sewn on the back—are pariahs of the highways. Not even flea-bag motels open to them, and they are forced to camp off the road.

The camping scenes form part of the structural welding points for the trek. On the first night out, Wyatt and Billy, strung out high on grass, their bikes behind them like tethered horses, stare at the campfire. "Out here in the wilderness fighting Indians and cowboys on every side," Billy jokes in his pot-head style. The scene fixes the "Western" context of the action: the two friends are indeed surrounded by savages and wild human animals.

Like the several camping sequences, the general movement of episodes in *Easy Rider* has a thematic and structural direction: events are not interchangeable as in most picaresque adventures but form a coherent pattern. The course of the action is from joy to disaster, and the points along the curve interlock, creating a surface cohesion. The theme of time is reticulated throughout. Before starting out on the journey, Wyatt, in a gesture closely resembling the young hunter's in Faulkner's "The Bear," deliberately leaves his watch behind. The ambiguous gesture's meaning is picked up later, when he must choose between continuing the trip—a rather pointless one, except for the promise of excitement at Mardi Gras—and staying at a hippie commune. "Your time is running out," a communard cautions him. For Wyatt the choice is clear: to ride is to try to keep ahead of time; to remain with the commune is to connect with himself and live fully within time. "I'm hip about time," he says, "but I've got to go."

To move or stay put. Wyatt dwells in the limbo of these alternatives. It speaks for the extraordinary intelligence of the director, Dennis Hopper, that this dilemma is interpreted visually. Wyatt, like the archetypal laconic Western hero, says little, but the camera records his staring at an old bucket, a worn paperback, or catches him alone, looking out across mountain stretches, as if he were trying to locate himself in things, time, space. Billy, by contrast, is all maniacal motion, giggling, high, pausing only to light the next joint. There is no need to know more about Wyatt; he is a condition, an inarticulate American Hamlet, as authentic to his milieu as Ishmael or Raskolnikof are to theirs.

Wyatt simply *is*: *Easy Rider* does not explain or justify how he can commit an immoral act (sell cocaine) and still be an ethical hero. Even heroes make mistakes in judgment, do not see their self-defeating or self-contradicting choices. The very premise of making a fortune in order to be free is Wyatt and Billy's basic fallacy. Wyatt understands this toward the end of the journey, and when Billy gloats over their success, he tells him, "We blew it." Yet ethics are a crucial concern of the film: considerate and polite behavior, with courtesy and fundamental human decencies. Wyatt is the exemplary hero, considerate, straight-forward, as are all the "good men" in the film. (A communard urges Billy to be "a trifle polite," to show respect for the Indians buried under their camp site.) For all his drooping Buffalo Bill moustache, Billy is really a pushy Easterner: he keeps his hat on at a rancher's supper until asked to remove it; he violates the unwritten code of the West by insistently asking a stranger's place of origin. Oblivious to forms of conduct, Billy is blind to the underlying harmony of the commune, too bent on buying freedom to see that he is in the same bag with any closed-off middle class dude.

The impulse in American culture running parallel yet counter to the road-movement-frontier tropism is the agrarian-settlement-commune, the drop-out and dig-in spirit which expressed itself in the Brook Farm, Oneida and Shaker communities in the American 1840's and 50's, or in the more lonely, individualistic setting of Thoreau's Walden experiment. The 1960's re-established the pattern with its drop-out cities in the Southwest, its New York City, Lower East Side commune and tribes. Not to do but to be is what the commune means: not to escape but to redefine oneself and to connect with others, to work out a pattern of personal and community destiny.

In *Easy Rider* glamour and ostensible freedom are expressed in the life of the open road, while everything that Wyatt and Billy seek are found in the values of the ranch and the desert commune they pass through.

"You do your own thing in your own time, you should be proud," Wyatt praises the rancher who has made roots with his Indian wife and children in an arid land. The rancher is a man who has made it—neither a victim nor an exploiter, he does not try or need to buy time in order to be free; he lives within time self-sufficiently, and more importantly, with love. Located pacifically in the center of all the violence in the film, the rancher and the values he represents—politeness, dignity, self-reliance—indicate a direction of being for Wyatt and are at the core of the film's yearning for an earlier, pastoral America.

However attractive the rancher and his family are as an idea, they are not figures for Wyatt and Billy to emulate. In immediate, generational terms, the rancher belongs to the survival, 19th century culture: for Wyatt and Billy, the desert commune represents a more viable counterpart to the ranch.

The commune is an extension of the rancher's family unit: many young families merged into one family. The commune represents Wyatt's generation's attempt to do in a conscious fashion what the rancher had arrived at organically, and it incorporates into the traditional 19th century structure its own generation's special ethos: drugs, sexual freedom, and an attire that once would have passed for costume.

As the commune scene is at the center of the film's nostalgic values, the desert commune episode is the pivotal point of Wyatt's fate. The commune is the vital alternative to Wyatt's wandering. It is the place for him to make his stand and connect. Wyatt is pulled toward remaining there and he is almost conscious of the fatality and suicide in his decision to race on to Mardi Gras. It is here that the film comes closest to a dimension of tragedy. Wyatt is a tragic figure who misses the mark and loses himself. His death is just a part of the toll of his being an outsider in an enemy culture, but his negation of what touched so deeply in life is his tragedy.

Easy Rider's strategy is founded on the paranoiac dread that innocence is crowded out, exterminated, like the buffalo. Billy and Wyatt belong to the ethos of the good, to the other America, victimized and lonely. And if the film is too easily prone to the pieties of martyrdom, it is a martyrdom that we all have witnessed in recent history, only we have lived with it as numbing spectacle, on large scale. Billy and Wyatt are diminutive models—backroads victims—of the grand design of national disaster. *Easy Rider* attempts to deal with existentialist issues in a national context, and as such, it is either a harbinger of some near future cataclysm or a paradigm of what has already occurred.

Easy Rider

the complete screenplay by

PETER FONDA
DENNIS HOPPER
TERRY SOUTHERN

(Running time 94 minutes.)

*Ls—ext La Contenta bar—day—*WYATT *and* BILLY *enter fg on motorcycles—they travel bg to front of cantina and stop at door—several Mexican men enter through door.*

WYATT: Buenas dias. (Good morning.)

MEN: *(Ad lib in Spanish.)* Bueno Amigos. Han denito a visitar? (All right, friends. You come here to visit?)

Ad lib indistinct chatter.

MAN: Vamos amigos. (Come on, friends.)

Cut to: mcs—Mexican leaning on crate looking off Left fg.

Abbreviations

fg	foreground	ls	long shot
bg	background	cs or cus	close shot or
ext	exterior		close up shot
int	interior	ms	medium shot
cam	camera	mcs	medium close shot
pov	point of view	mls	medium long shot
os	off-screen	els	extended long shot

MAN: *(os)* Vamos a mirar. (Let's go and look.)

Cut to: ms—shooting over pile of junk to three Mexicans looking fg.

MAN: *(os)* Jesus, mira a nuestros amigos. (Jesus, look at our friends.)

Cut to: mls—BILLY and WYATT standing at rear of cantina with Mexican and little girl—JESUS and another Mexican move out from rear door to greet them.

JESUS: Dios bendiga. Como esta? Eh? Garay! Crei que no vendrias. (God bless. How are you? Eh? Gosh! I thought you were not coming.)

WYATT: De veras? (Really?)

JESUS: Si. Los caballos siempre dicen que van a venir. Puras alas. Pero nunca vienen. (Yes. The horses always said that they will come. A lot of hooey. But they never come.)

WYATT: Pues, aqui estamos. (Well, here we are.)

Pan Left as JESUS and WYATT walk bg Left, followed by BILLY and others and bringing in three Mexicans leaning against junk watching—stop pan and dolly Left as group moves bg into auto wrecking dump.

JESUS: Oye ya los plante. (You know, I left them flat.)

Ad lib indistinct chatter.

Cut to: mcs—ext wrecking dump—WYATT facing Right—BILLY behind Left—group of Mexicans in bg —pan Right past BILLY as WYATT moves Right bringing in JESUS behind him—tilt down and hold JESUS ms as WYATT fg stops and stoops down, back to cam —JESUS stoops down—BILLY enters Left.

*Cut to: cs—*BILLY *stoops down facing Right fg—pan slightly Right bringing in* JESUS *partially Right.*

*Cut to: cs—*WYATT *facing Left fg.*

*Cut to: ms—*JESUS *between* BILLY *and* WYATT—*he scoops out white powder from small case and taps it onto mirror held by* WYATT—WYATT *brings mirror up to his nose.*

*Cut to: cs—*WYATT *holding mirror to his nose—he sniffs powder.*

WYATT: *(Sniffs.)*

He lowers mirror and holds it out fg os. cut to: cs— BILLY—WYATT's *hand in fg holding mirror—*BILLY *takes mirror, holds it to his nose and sniffs powder—* WYATT's *hand withdraws—*JESUS *in Right.*

BILLY: *(Sniffs.)*

*Cut to: cs—*WYATT *looks fg, raises eyebrows.*

*Cut to: cs—*BILLY—JESUS *tipped in Right.*

BILLY: *(Chuckles.)*

*Cut to: ms—*BILLY, JESUS *and* WYATT—WYATT *tastes powder on his finger.*

BILLY: *(Gasps.)*

*Cut to: cs—*JESUS.

JESUS: Esta mal, Hermano. Por la vida, Hermano. (It's not good, Brother. For the life, Brother.)

*Cut to: cs—*WYATT *smiling.*

WYATT: *(Chuckles.)* Si, pura vida. (Yes, it's pure life.)

43

Cut to: cs—BILLY—JESUS tipped in Right.

BILLY: Bueno. *(Laughs.)*

> BILLY *claps* JESUS *on shoulder.*
>
> *Cut to: cs—WYATT—he reaches below frame into his pocket, takes out something and hands it fg os.*
>
> *Cut to: ms—BILLY and JESUS—WYATT Right fg, back to cam—WYATT hands packet of money to JESUS—JESUS thumbs through it, smiles and nods.*

JESUS: Dame esa. Parece que esta todo. (Give me that. It seems like that's everything.)

> *Mexican leans in Left, hands small case to JESUS and leans os—JESUS hands case to WYATT—BILLY closes first case.*

BILLY: Muchas gracias. (Thank you.)

> *The three rise, heads os.*

JESUS: Bueno. (All right.) Ya sabe que siempre bienvenido. (You know you're always welcome.)

WYATT: Muchas gracias. (Thank you.)

> *Cut to: ms—shooting over pile of junk to three Mexicans.*

JESUS: *(os)* Eh?

WYATT: *(os)* Muchas gracias.

JESUS: *(os)* Bueno. (All right.)
> *Pan Left past the three to ms of fat man and little*

girl.

*Cut to: cs—ext airport—day—*WYATT *looking up fg smiling—airstrip bg—*WYATT *turns bg as jet enters fg over top frame and flies low bg to land on airstrip.*

Cut to: ls—low angle: jet approaches.

*Cut to: mls—ext airport road—*WYATT *standing on bumper of pickup truck, looking skyward—*BILLY *at rear of pickup, crouched down and holding his ears —jet enters fg over top frame, flies bg and exits behind fence—front end of Rolls Royce enters Right fg and stops—*BILLY *straightens.*

Cut to: cs—ext Rolls Royce—shooting through passenger side window at THE CONNECTION *in back seat reaching bg, back to cam—*BODYGUARD'S *reflection in window—*THE CONNECTION *turns and looks fg out window.*

Cut to: mls—shooting across hood of Rolls to BODY-GUARD *opening passenger door—*THE CONNECTION *enters from car—pan Left as he crosses Left, followed by* BODYGUARD, *and enters to* BILLY *and* WYATT *at side of pickup—*WYATT *and* THE CONNECTION *shake hands—pan Left as the four move Left to truck's door—stop and hold the four mls as they crouch and hold their ears as jet enters above frame fg and flies bg to exit behind fence—*WYATT *opens truck door—*THE CONNECTION, *bag in hand, makes to get into truck.*

*Cut to: cs—int pickup truck—*THE CONNECTION *gets fg into truck—*WYATT *enters behind as he closes door—*WYATT *exits Right—*THE CONNECTION, *reaching Right os, adjusts rearview mirror—he looks at himself, adjusts cap on his head and brushes down sideburns.*

*Cut to: mls—ext airport road—*BODYGUARD *and* BILLY *at side of pickup truck—*WYATT *moves bg around front of truck to passenger side.*

*Cut to: cs—*BILLY *looking fg.*

*Cut to: cs—*DRIVER *facing Right.*

*Cut to: mcs—*THE CONNECTION *in pickup, seen through driver's window, back to cam—*WYATT *bg on passenger side, seen through window—*BILLY *and* DRIVER *reflected Left fg in rearview mirror—favors* BILLY.

*Cut to: cs—int pickup—*THE CONNECTION *looking down fg—pan slightly Right as he turns bg, bringing in jet approaching and* DRIVER's *reflection in rearview mirror—pan down Left past* BODYGUARD *and jet as* THE CONNECTION *crouches down Left fg, putting hands over his head.*

*Cut to: cs—ext truck—*BILLY *winces and puts fingers to his ears.*

*Cut to: cs—int truck—*WYATT *looking in fg through window.*

Cut to: mcs—int pickup—high angle: THE CONNECTION *crouched over, hands to his ears—two small*

46

*cases open on seat, filled with white powder—leather bag beside them—*THE CONNECTION *lowers his hands and dips small spoon into powder.*

*Cut to: cs—*WYATT *looking in fg through window.*

*Cut to: cus—*THE CONNECTION *holds small spoonful of powder to his nose and sniffs.*

*Cut to: cs—*WYATT *looking in fg through window, smiles.*

*Cut to: cus—*THE CONNECTION *sniffs powder, cocks his head and smiles.*

*Cut to: cs—*WYATT *looking in fg through window.*

*Cut to: cs—*THE CONNECTION *looks up fg and smiles and holds out spoon.*

*Cut to: cus—*WYATT *smiling, shakes his head.*

*Cut to: cs—*THE CONNECTION *smiles and shrugs.*

*Cut to: mcs—ext pickup—*THE CONNECTION *seen through side window, back to cam—*WYATT *bg on passenger side, seen through window—*BILLY *and* BODYGUARD *reflected Left in rearview mirror—*THE CONNECTION *turns fg holding the two cases—pan Right past reflections in mirror as* THE CONNECTION *holds cases fg out window—*BODYGUARD *enters Right fg and takes them—he steps back os—pan Left bringing in* BODYGUARD *and* BILLY *reflected in mirror as* THE CONNECTION *turns bg—*BODYGUARD'S *reflection exits as he moves out—*THE CONNECTION *nods at* WYATT *as he puts on gloves.*

*Cut to: mls—ext Rolls Royce—*DRIVER *leaning into car from passenger side—*BILLY *enters Left and moves Right to stand behind* DRIVER—WYATT *enters Left and moves Right to* BILLY—DRIVER *straightens from car holding packet of money—he slaps* BILLY'S *hands away and hands money to* WYATT—WYATT *gets into front seat and counts money—*DRIVER *closes door and steps back Left—*THE CONNECTION *enters bg Left—*BILLY *opens back seat door and* THE CONNECTION *gets in.*

*Cut to: ls—*BILLY *and* DRIVER *at side of Rolls—*BILLY *opens car door and* WYATT *gets out—*BILLY *and* WYATT *move Left fg and exit.*

Cut to: ls—ext desert—day—pickup enters bg on road—cam dollies Left to road as pickup approaches —zoom back and pan Left with pickup—stop and hold els, sun setting behind mountain as pickup exits Left—zoom in.

Music over—"The Pusher."

Cut to: cus—cam pans up motorcycle and plastic tube holding rolled-up money, bringing in cus of WYATT *as he rolls up banknotes and stuffs roll into tube—he corks up end of tube.*

Cut to: cus—motorcycle gas tank as WYATT'S *hands feed plastic tube holding money into tank—pull back to cs as he puts on cap.*

*Cut to: cus—*WYATT'S *hand screwing on cap.*

*Cut to: scene blurred—scene clears showing cs of motorcycle tire—pan up Right along handles of cycle to starred-and-striped helmet—*WYATT's *hand enters and picks up helmet—pan up to cs of* WYATT *as he raises helmet up, brushes it off and straps it onto bar of cycle—he turns Left and bends down os.*

*Cut to: mls—ext deserted building—day—*WYATT *enters Right behind wall on motorcycle—pan Left as he rides Left to rock formations and stops—hold him ms facing Left—*BILLY *enters Right and pulls up beside him—*WYATT *looks at wristwatch and takes it off.*

*Cut to: cus—*WYATT *looking at wristwatch—zoom back to cs and in to cus as he lowers watch os.*

*Cut to: ms—*WYATT *and* BILLY*—zoom back to mls.*

*Cut to: cus—*WYATT *looking down Right.*

Cut to: cs—high angle: WYATT's *watch on ground.*

Cut to: mls—pan Left as WYATT *rides Left onto road, followed by* BILLY*—they travel bg.*

Fade in superimposed title: PANDO COMPANY in association with RAYBERT PRODUCTIONS presents

Fade out title.

Cut to: cs—ext desert road—day—cam trucks back as WYATT *rides Left on motorcycle.*

Fade in superimposed title: PETER FONDA

Fade out title.

Cut to: mcs—cam trucks back as WYATT *rides Left—*BILLY *enters Right fg alongside.*

Cut to: cs—cam trucks back as BILLY *rides Left fg—pan Left with him bringing in* WYATT *bg alongside him—pan Left past* BILLY *as* WYATT *pulls ahead—*BILLY *enters Right fg.*

Fade in superimposed title: DENNIS HOPPER

Fade out title.

Cut to: els—ext road—day—bridge spanning river

in bg—cam trucks Left holding on bridge, passing sign reading: Colorado River.

Music over—"Born to be Wild."

Cut to: cs—moving shot: WYATT *riding Right fg, smiles.*

Cut to: cs—moving shot: BILLY *riding fg, smiling.*

Cut to: ms—moving shot: WYATT *riding Left—*BILLY *bg alongside, takes hands off handlebars—cam pulls ahead and pans Right to hold them ms.*

Fade in superimposed title: EASY RIDER—COPY-RIGHT (C) MCMLXIX BY RAYBERT PRO-DUCTIONS, INC. ALL RIGHTS RESERVED.

Cut to: mls—moving shot: cam zooms back from bridge to hold it ls.

Cut to: mls—cam trucks in behind WYATT *and* BILLY *riding by passing sign that reads: Arizona State Line —cam zooms back.*

Fade out above superimposed title.

Cut to: els—cam trucks Left holding on bridge bg spanning Colorado River.

Cut to: ms—running insert: WYATT *riding Left fg followed by* BILLY*—pan Left as they pull up Left fg.*

Fade in superimposed title: STARRING *(In alpha-betical order)*

Fade out title.

Cut to: mls—shooting through wire divider fence to WYATT *and* BILLY *riding to Left—zoom back to ls.*

Fade in superimposed title: LUANA ANDERS

Title fades out.

Title fades in: LUKE ASKEW

Title fades out.

Title fades in: TONI BASIL

Title fades out.

Title fades in: KAREN BLACK

Title fades out.

*Cut to: mls—*BILLY *and* WYATT *riding fg up sloping road—zoom back and pan Left as they ride Left and bg along road.*

Fade in superimposed title: WARREN FINNERTY

Fade out title.

Fade in title: SABRINA SCHARF

Fade out title.

Fade in title: ROBERT WALKER

Fade out title.

Cut to: ls—ext road—running insert: BILLY *and* WYATT *approaching on cycles.*

Fade in superimposed title: AND JACK NICHOLSON AS GEORGE HANSON

Fade out title.

Cut to: ls—low angle: moving shot from their pov as they ride bg under overpass.

Cut to: mls—ext Flagstaff—cam trucks back Left as WYATT *and* BILLY *ride Left past giant statue of miner.*

Cut to: mls—ext Flagstaff—shooting from their pov cam trucks in toward hotel on corner.

Cut to: ms—cam trucks back Right as WYATT *and* BILLY *ride to Right—*WYATT *pulls ahead—*BILLY *moves up beside him.*

Fade in superimposed title:
Film Editor: DONN CAMBERN

All characters depicted in this Photoplay are fictitious. Any similarity to actual persons, living or dead, is purely coincidental.

Fade out title.

Cut to: ms—cam trucks back and pans Left with WYATT *and* BILLY *as they ride Left to intersection.*

Fade in superimposed title:
Assistant Editor: STANLEY SIEGEL
Consultant: HENRY JAGLOM
Sound Effects: EDIT-RITE, INC.

Music Editing: SYNCHROFILM, INC.
Re-recording: PRODUCER'S SOUND SERVICE, INC.
Sound: RYDER SOUND SERVICE, INC.
Titles: CINEFX
Color Processing: CONSOLIDATED FILM IN-DUSTRIES
*Approved   No. 22175 (emblem) MOTION PIC-*TURE ASSOCIATION OF AMERICA

Cut to: ls—cam trucks Left on road holding on train-yard—boxcar on side track marked: Sante Fe.

Fade out superimposed title.

*Cut to: cam trucks in along white line that stretches bg down deserted road—*BILLY *enters Left—*WYATT *Right—they ride bg.*

Fade in superimposed title:
Art Director: JERRY KAY
Assistant Cameraman: PETER HEISER, JR.
Sound Mixer: LE ROY ROBBINS
Gaffer: RICHMOND AGUILAR
Key Grip: THOMAS RAMSEY
Script Supervisor: JOYCE KING
Location Manager: TONY VORNO
Transportation: LEE PIERPONT
Post Production: MARILYN SCHLOSSBERG

Fade out title.

*Cut to: ls—*WYATT *and* BILLY *approach—pan Left as they ride fg and Left bg.*

Fade in superimposed title:
Second Assistant-Director: LEN MARSAL
Prop Master: ROBERT O'NEIL
Make-up: VIRGIL FRYE
Special Effects: STEVE KARKUS
Still Man: PETER SOREL
Electrician: FOSTER DENKER
Best Boy: MEL MAXWELL
Sound Boom: JAMES CONTRARES
Generator: GUY BADGER
Stunt Gaffer: TEX HALL

Fade out superimposed title.

Cut to: ls—ext gas station/motel—night—two head-lights approach from bg—they turn Right off road to motel.

Fade in superimposed title: PRODUCTION MAN-AGER: PAUL LEWIS

Title fades out.

Title fades in: ASSOCIATE PRODUCER: WIL-LIAM L. HAYWARD

Title fades out.

Cut to: mls—ext motel—WYATT and BILLY enter Right—pan Right as WYATT rides fg and pulls up to face Right—hold him ms—BILLY pulls up bg before motel door and honks horn—neon light goes on read-ing: Vacancy.

Fade in superimposed title: DIRECTOR OF PHO-TOGRAPHY: LASZLO KOVACS

Fade out title.

Fade in title: EXECUTIVE PRODUCER: BERT SCHNEIDER

Title fades out.

Title fades in: WRITTEN BY: PETER FONDA—. DENNIS HOPPER—TERRY SOUTHERN

Title fades out.

Proprietor enters through door.

WYATT: Hey, you got a room?

Proprietor turns and exits back into office.

WYATT: Hey, man! You gotta room?

Fade in title: PRODUCED BY PETER FONDA
Title fades out.

Another neon light goes on over first sign—it reads: No—WYATT exits as he backs cycle Left os.

Fade in title: DIRECTED BY: DENNIS HOPPER
Fade out title.

Pan Left as BILLY *wheels cycle fg and Left, bringing in* WYATT *turning bg—stop and hold them mls as they ride bg to road—*BILLY *gives "the finger."*

WYATT *seated before open fire.*

Cut to: Flash cuts of BILLY *and* WYATT *seated on ground before open fire and traveling bg away from motel.*

*Cut to: mls—ext campsite—night—*BILLY *and* WYATT *seated before open fire.*

BILLY: *(Sings.)*
 "I'm goin' down to Mardi Gras
 I'm gonna get me a Mardi Gras queen. . . ."
 Yeah. Oh, man. Wow! Mardi Gras, man. That's gonna be
 the weirdest, man, you know.

WYATT: Hmmm.

BILLY: Whew!

> *Cut to: ms*—BILLY *and* WYATT.

BILLY: You know what we ought to do, man? The first thing—
go and get us a groovy dinner. Yeah. Break out some of that
cash, man.

> *Cut to: mls—ext campsite—night*—BILLY *and*
> WYATT *seated before open fire.*

BILLY: *(Howls.)* Out here in the wilderness, fighting Indians
and cowboys on every side. Ah.

> *Cut to: ms*—BILLY *and* WYATT.

BILLY: Uhmmm. What's the matter, you zonked . . . what?
Huh—you really zonked, eh?

WYATT: No, I'm—uh—just kind of tired.

BILLY: Yeah, man—you're pulling inside, man. You're getting a little distance tonight. *(Chuckles.)* You're getting a little distance, man.

WYATT: Yeah, well, I'm just getting my thing together.

> *Cut to: flash cuts:* BILLY *and* WYATT *in field to int shed, low angle: sky seen through broken slat in roof.*

> *Cut to: mls—int shed—morning—low angle: sun flickering through broken slats in roof—cam dollies Left.*

> *Cut to: cs—ext field—day—cam pans Right as* WYATT *walks slowly Right looking skyward.*

> *Cut to: ms—int broken-down shed.*

> *Cut to: mcs—high angle: branches shadowed on shed floor.*

> *Cut to: cs—bush—its shadow behind on floor of shed.*

> *Cut to: ms—high angle: rusted piece of tin on ground.*

> *Cut to: mls—cam dollies in toward broken-down shed.*

> *Cut to: mls—ext field—wreck of car—pan slightly Right.*

> *Cut to: cs—*WYATT *leaning against post—he looks up fg.*

> *Cut to: ms—int shed—low angle: sun flickering through broken roof.*

> *Cut to: mcs—ext field—high angle: drawer on ground with rusted compass and withered piece of paper inside—*WYATT's *shadow enters Right on ground—pan up Right past drawer to* WYATT *stooping down looking at booklet—hold him mcs high angle: back to cam—he opens booklet and breeze flips pages—pan up as he rises and turns fg—pan Right as he crosses bg Right bringing in deserted shed as he walks bg and enters to* BILLY *on ground asleep.*

*Cut to: ms—*WYATT *standing over* BILLY *asleep on ground.*

WYATT: Come on, it's checkout time, Hey! Billy!

WYATT *kicks* BILLY's *foot—*BILLY *wakes and jumps to his feet.*

BILLY: Oh, man—don't do that. Whew!

Cut to: ls—shooting through chicken-coop fence at BILLY *on cycle—pan as he rides Left between shed and coop and enters to* WYATT *on cycle—they ride bg and exit behind shack as two children enter bg riding horse.*

*Cut to: ls—ext farm—day—*BILLY *riding slowly fg alongside* WYATT *wheeling his cycle with flat tire— pan Right as they move Right bringing in children fg.*

*Cut to: ls—*BILLY *and* WYATT *approaching.*

Cut to: els—ext farmhouse yard—shooting across yard to BILLY *and* WYATT *moving Right along farm road.*

*Cut to: mls—two farmers shoeing horse—*WYATT *enters Right fg wheeling cycle—he stops, back to cam.*

RANCHER: Howdy. What can I do for you?

WYATT: I'd like to fix my flat, if you don't mind.

RANCHER: No, I don't mind.

*Cut to: mcs—*RANCHER *holding horse's head.*

RANCHER: Just get in the barn there. You'll find any tools you'll need.

Horse pulls its head back.

RANCHER: Whoa, baby. Whoa, honey. Now turn that thing off.
   You're making my horse skittish.

> *Cut to: mcs—low angle: second farmer leaning on
> horse.*

> *Cut to: mls—two farmers Left—*BILLY *and* WYATT
> *Right, wheel motorcycles bg into barn and exit.*

RANCHER: That sure is a good-looking machine.

> *Cut to: mls—int barn—*BILLY *and* WYATT *enter Left
> wheeling cycle—they halt.*

WYATT: Yeah.

> *Cut to: mcs—ext yard—low angle: second farmer
> leaning on horse.*

> *Cut to: mls—int. barn—*BILLY *and* WYATT *prop up
> rear wheel of cycle.*

> *Cut to: ms—ext yard—high angle:* RANCHER *kneel-
> ing, pounding on horseshoe—second farmer in bg,
> waist down in scene.*

> *Cut to: ms—int barn—*WYATT *and* BILLY *take off
> rear tire.*

> *Ad lib gasps and grunts.*

WYATT: (*Coughs.*)

> *Cut to: ms—ext yard—*RANCHER *putting shoe on
> horse—second farmer behind him—*WYATT *and*
> BILLY *bg in barn working on cycle.*

RANCHER: (*Gasps.*) There you go.

> *Cut to: mls—ext farmhouse—day—*BILLY *and* WYATT
> *at table washing up—*RANCHER, *workers and family*

*seated bg at table—*BILLY *and* WYATT *move bg through gateway to join them.*

RANCHER: Here, you fellas can sit down here.

Cam dollies in to hold mls as BILLY *and* WYATT *sit on either side of* RANCHER *at head of table.*

BILLY: Oh-ho!

Cut to: mcs—shooting from behind WYATT *to* BILLY *across table as he takes bite of food.*

RANCHER: *(os)* Would you mind—uh—taking off your hat?

BILLY *looks to Left.*

Cut to: ms—shooting from BILLY's *pov to woman and little girl seated at table, hands folded and heads bowed.*

Cut to: mcs—shooting from behind WYATT *to* BILLY *—he takes off his hat and folds his hands—cam dollies Left along table past men, women and children seated fg and bg at table, hands folded, heads bowed.*

RANCHER: *(os)* Ahem. We thank Thee, O Lord for these Thy gifts received from Thy bounty in the name of Thy only begotten Son, Jesus Christ, Our Lord. Amen.

*Cut to: cs—*RANCHER*—he takes false teeth out of his mouth and puts them in his pocket.*

*Cut to: cs—*WYATT *eating.*

*Cut to: cs—*RANCHER.

RANCHER: Where are you fellas from?

WYATT: *(os)* L.A.

RANCHER: L.A.?

Cut to: cs—WYATT.

WYATT: Los Angeles. *(Sniffs.)*

RANCHER: *(os)* Los Angeles. Is that a fact? When I was a young man I was—

Cut to: cs—RANCHER.

RANCHER: —headed for California. But—well, you know how it is.

Cut to: cs—BILLY.

Cut to: cs—WYATT *looks about.*

WYATT: Well, you sure got a nice spread here.

Cut to: cs—RANCHER.

RANCHER: Yeah, I sure got a lot of 'em. My wife's Catholic, you know.

Cut to: cs—RANCHER'S WIFE *looking to Left.*

BILLY: *(os)* *(Laughs.)*

Cut to: cs—RANCHER *facing Right.*

RANCHER: Honey, can we have some more coffee?

Cut to: cs—RANCHER'S WIFE *nods, rises and turns bg.*

Cut to: cs—WYATT.

WYATT: No, I mean it. You've got a nice place. It's not every man that can live off the land, you know. You do your own thing in your own time. You should be proud.

Cut to: mls—ext road—day—low angle: cam trucks in along trees as sun flickers through branches of tree-lined road.

Cut to: mls—low angle: cam trucks back from trees as sunlight flickers through.

Cut to: els—cam trucks Right holding on hills—pan Left to ms of WYATT *riding Right—*BILLY's *hands fg on handles of cycle—he pulls in—pan Right as they ride bg to hold them ms, backs to cam.*

Music over—"Wasn't Born to Follow."

Cut to: ms—cam trucks in behind BILLY *and* WYATT *riding bg.*

Cut to: ls—cam trucks in Left along road, holding on wooded area.

Cut to: els—cam trucks in along deserted road—pan Left to wooded area.

Cut to: mcs—moving camera on BILLY *riding to Right—*WYATT *bg alongside.*

Cut to: ms—Cam trucks back as BILLY *and* WYATT *ride fg—*BILLY *points off Right.*

Cut to: els—shooting from their pov to woods and mountains as cam trucks Right.

Cut to: ms—cam trucks back Right as BILLY *and* WYATT *ride Right fg.*

Cut to: mls—cam trucks back as BILLY *and* WYATT *ride fg into ms.*

Cut to: mcs—cam trucks back as WYATT *rides fg.*

Cut to: els—shooting from behind STRANGER *standing Left in road, back to cam, to* BILLY *and* WYATT *approaching—*STRANGER *puts out thumb.*

*Cut to: mls—*BILLY *and* WYATT *riding Left by* STRANGER *in road—*BILLY *exits Left as* WYATT *stops and makes to turn cycle around.*

Cut to: mcs—low angle: STRANGER *facing Left.*

Cut to: mls—pan Left as WYATT *cycles Left bringing in* STRANGER *Left fg, back to cam—hold mls as* WYATT *turns cycle around and wheels up to* STRANGER—BILLY *enters Right and joins them as* STRANGER *gets onto cycle behind* WYATT—*pan Right as they ride Right fg and bg.*

Cut to: cs—cam holding on WYATT *as he rides Left— pan Right bringing in* STRANGER *behind him—zoom back to ms—pan Right past them to* BILLY *following.*

Cut to: mls—cam trucks back as WYATT *and* STRANGER *ride fg followed by* BILLY.

*Cut to: ls—*BILLY, WYATT *and* STRANGER *approach— mountains bg capped with snow—pan Right as they pull bg Right off road to Enco gas station—lettering on building reads: Sacred Mountain.*

*Cut to: ms—ext Enco gas station—*WYATT *and* STRANGER *on motorcycle—they get off—pan Left*

past WYATT *as* STRANGER *moves Left, enters to* BILLY *on cycle, and takes down gas hose—hold them mls as* BILLY *gets off cycle and takes hose from* STRANGER *—pan Right past* BILLY *as* STRANGER *moves Right bringing in* WYATT *fg in ms—*STRANGER *takes down gas hose—*WYATT *turns bg and removes gas cap.*

Cut to: cs—low angle: STRANGER *bends down fg.*

Cut to: mcs—high angle: STRANGER's *hands holding gas pump into cycle's gas tank.*

Cut to: cs—low angle: STRANGER *bending down.*

BILLY: (*os*) Hey, man, what are you doing?

STRANGER *looks up Left.*

*Cut to: ms—*BILLY *and* WYATT*—*STRANGER *behind.*

BILLY: Hey c'mon. I gotta talk to you, man.

Dolly back and pan Left past STRANGER *as* BILLY *and* WYATT *move to Left.*

BILLY: Whew.

They stop and face each other—hold them mcs.

BILLY: Hey, man—everything that we ever dreamed of is in that teardrop gas tank—and you got a stranger over there pouring gasoline all over it, man. All he's got to do is turn and look over into it, man, and he can see that—

WYATT: He won't know what it is, man. He won't know what it is. Don't worry, Billy. Everything's all right.

BILLY: Yeah, man. All right. I don't know, man.

WYATT: I do. Everything's fine, Billy.

WYATT takes out money—pan Right past BILLY *and dolly in as* WYATT *crosses bg Right and enters to* STRANGER *at gas pump—stop and hold them ms as* STRANGER *takes hose from tank and* WYATT *puts cap on tank—*STRANGER *puts away hose and steps back to* WYATT*—*WYATT *holds out money.*

WYATT: Well, uh-huh—

STRANGER: That's all taken care of.

WYATT: I like that. (*Chuckles.*)

Cut to: mls—ext gas station building—Mexican girl looking fg out window.

*Cut to: ls—ext road—day—*BILLY, WYATT *and* STRANGER *ride bg from gas station.*

*Cut to: ls—*BILLY, WYATT *and* STRANGER *pull away*

from gas station—they ride fg and exit.

Cut to: ms—ext road—High angle: cam trucks in along painted lines in center of road.

Cut to: mls—cam zooms back and trucks in behind BILLY, WYATT *and* STRANGER *as they ride bg.*

Cut to: mls—cam trucks in Left and pans Left past WYATT *and* STRANGER *as* BILLY *pulls bg ahead of them.*

Music over—"The Weight."

Cut to: els—cam trucks in Right along road holding on mountains—tilt down Left as BILLY *rides in Left.*

Cut to: mcs—high angle: trucking in Left with cycle wheeling Left—pan Left bringing in feet of STRANGER *and* WYATT.

Cut to: els—pan Left as BILLY, WYATT *and* STRANGER *ride Left along road.*

Cut to: mls—cam trucks back as BILLY, WYATT *and* STRANGER *ride Left fg.*

Cut to: ms—Cam trucks back Left as WYATT *and* BILLY *ride Left—*BILLY *drops back bg Right as* WYATT *pulls ahead, bringing in* STRANGER *behind him—zoom back to mls as* BILLY *pulls across to Right—*STRANGER *points off Right.*

Cut to: els—cam trucks Right holding on open terrain.

Cut to: els—cam trucks Right holding onto sun setting on horizon.

Cut to: ls—cam trucks Left holding on rocky terrain.

Cut to: els—pointed rock on top of plateau silhouetted against sky.

Cut to: els—rock formation silhouetted against sky.

Cut to: ls—cam trucks back as WYATT, STRANGER *and* BILLY *ride fg.*

Cut to: els—cam trucks Left holding on plateau—pan Left bringing in BILLY, WYATT *and* STRANGER *riding bg down road.*

*Cut to: mls—*WYATT, STRANGER *and* BILLY *approaching, camera trucking back.*

Cut to: els—multicolored sky—pan Right along high plateaus and rock formations.

*Cut to: mls—ext desert—night—*BILLY, STRANGER *and* WYATT *on parked cycles—they get off—pan Right as* WYATT *walks to Right.*

*Cut to: mls—*WYATT, STRANGER *and* BILLY *walk to rock formation.*

*Cut to: mls—*BILLY *and* WYATT *enter from behind rock formation—tilt up as they climb up to top and stand silhouetted against evening sky—*STRANGER *enters behind rock and stops.*

Cut to: flash cuts of the three on rock formation and ruins.

*Cut to: mls—ext ruins—night—*BILLY, STRANGER *and* WYATT *seated before open fire.*

BILLY: How much farther do we got to go, man?

WYATT: I don't know.

BILLY: Huh?

STRANGER: Not much further.

BILLY: (*Laughs.*) That's what you said this mornin'.

Cut to: cs—STRANGER.

STRANGER: I sometimes say it all day.

BILLY: (*os*) (*Laughs.*) You say it all day. (*Coughs.*)

STRANGER: We don't have much longer. We'll be there soon.

BILLY: (*os*) We gotta get to Mardi Gras, man. We're goin' to the Mardi Gras.

STRANGER: Your little heart is set on that, huh?

Cut to: cs—WYATT.

WYATT: We got a week.

Cut to: cs—STRANGER.

WYATT: (*os*) That's a week away, man.

BILLY: (*os*) It's a long way to Mardi Gras, baby.

Cut to: cs—WYATT.

WYATT: It won't take us a week to get to New Orleans.

Cut to: cs—STRANGER.
Cut to: cs—WYATT.

WYATT: Wow! I think I'm gonna crash.

BILLY: (os) (Laughs.) Ah, man.

> *Cut to: mls*—BILLY, STRANGER *and* WYATT—BILLY *rises.*

BILLY: I think you have crashed, man. (Chuckles.)

> *Cut to: cs*—STRANGER—BILLY *behind, moves Right and sits against wall.*

BILLY: Ahhhh!

> *Cut to: cs*—WYATT.

WYATT: (Sighs.)

> *Cut to: mcs*—STRANGER—WYATT *behind Right*—BILLY *in bg.*

WYATT: I keep seeing things jumping all over the place.

BILLY: (Laughs.) Really?

WYATT: Yeah, look—

> WYATT *picks up bug.*

WYATT: (Mutters indistinctly.) What is this—it's a moth.

BILLY: A what?

STRANGER: A moth. Bug.

> STRANGER *reaches out and* WYATT *puts bug in his hand.*

WYATT: (*Sniffs.*) Wow!

WYATT *takes off glasses and wipes his eyes.*

BILLY: It's a weird place, man.

WYATT: Oh, man. (*Sniffs.*) That smoke's getting to me. (*Sniffs.*)

STRANGER: I notice you're not moving.

Ad lib laughter.
Cut to: cs—STRANGER *smoking*—BILLY *in bg.*

Cut to: mcs—STRANGER—WYATT *behind Right*—
BILLY *in bg.*

BILLY: (*Addressing stranger.*) Where are you from, man?

WYATT: Can I—uh—can I have a light?

BILLY: Where you from, man?

STRANGER *hands joint to* WYATT, *who lights his from it.*

STRANGER: It's hard to say.

BILLY: (*Laughs.*) It's hard to say? Where you from, man?

STRANGER: Well, it's hard to say because it's a very long word, you know.

Cut to: cs—STRANGER *looking bg to* BILLY.

BILLY: I just want to know where you're from, man.

STRANGER *turns and looks down fg.*

STRANGER: (*Sighs.*) A city.

He turns to look bg at BILLY.

BILLY: Just a city?

STRANGER: Mmm-mmm.

STRANGER *turns and looks down fg.*

STRANGER: It doesn't make any difference what city. All cities are alike. That's why I'm out here now.

BILLY: (*Laughs.*) That's why you're out here now?

STRANGER: Yeah.

BILLY: Yeah, why?

STRANGER: 'Cause I'm from the city, a long way from the city —and that's where I want to be right now.

Cut to: cs—WYATT.

WYATT: Do they know you in this place? (*Sniffs.*)

Cut to: cs—STRANGER—BILLY *in bg.*

STRANGER: This place we're coming to?

WYATT: (*os*) No, here.

STRANGER: The place we're at now?

Cut to: cs—WYATT.

WYATT: This place. (*Laughs.*)

Cut to: cs—STRANGER—BILLY *in bg.*

BILLY: (*Laughs.*)

STRANGER *turns bg to* BILLY.

STRANGER: You're right on top of 'em.

BILLY: I'm right on top of 'em?

STRANGER: Yeah. The people this place belongs to are buried right under you.

STRANGER *turns fg.*

STRANGER: You could be a trifle polite.

BILLY: A trifle polite? (*Laughs.*)

STRANGER: A small thing to ask.

Cut to: cs—WYATT.

WYATT: You ever want to be somebody else?

Cut to: cs—STRANGER—BILLY *in bg.*

STRANGER: (*Sighs.*) I'd like to try Porky Pig.

Cut to: cs—WYATT.

WYATT: Mmmm! I never wanted to be anybody else.

Cut to: cs—STRANGER.

Cut to: cs—WYATT.

· *Cut to: flash cuts: cs* WYATT *and low angle: sun*

flickering through branches of tree—end of scene blurs.

Cut to: ms—ext road—day—cam trucks back Left as WYATT *and* STRANGER *ride to Left—*STRANGER *points ahead—*WYATT *nods.*

Cut to: mls—ext road—cam trucks in behind BILLY, WYATT *and* STRANGER *as they ride bg—pan Right past them to els of snow-capped mountains.*

Cut to: ls—ext river/Mexican village—day—pan Left as WYATT, STRANGER *and* BILLY *ride Left along bank and turn bg onto dirt road.*

Cut to: mls—pan Right as BILLY, WYATT *and* STRANGER *ride Right past cemetery in bg.*

Cut to: ls—shooting across river at BILLY, WYATT *and* STRANGER *riding into pueblo village.*

Cut to: ls—pan Right as WYATT, STRANGER *and* BILLY *ride bg Right through village.*

*Cut to: mls—ext commune—day—woman Right walking up slope carrying bucket—*WYATT, STRANGER *and* BILLY *enter bg Right on motorcycles—cam dollies back and pans Right as they ride up slope and Right to hippies gathered outside building—stop and hold mls as* WYATT *and* BILLY *park cycles.*

CHILDREN: (*Ad lib laughter and shouts.*)

CHILDREN *run forward to cycles as* STRANGER *gets off and moves bg Left.*

STRANGER: Hey, hey, hey, hey!

Cut to: ms—shooting from behind group of CHILDREN *as* STRANGER *steps to* LISA—*they kiss—he bends her down and kisses her more passionately.*

CHILDREN: (*Ad lib chatter and laughter.*) They're kissing.

*Cut to: cs—*WYATT *looking off Left.*

Indistinct chatter os.

*Cut to: ms—*BILLY *standing beside* SARAH—STRANGER *and* LISA *enter Left—*LISA *holding bag.*

CHILD: (*os*) He was kissing her. (*Laughs—indistinct shout.*)

*Cut to: ms—*WYATT *standing Right—*STRANGER *enters Left and turns fg.*

CHILDREN: (*os*) (*Ad lib chatter and laughter.*)

STRANGER: (*Sighs.*)

*He bends down fg to washbasin, flicks water in his face—*LISA *and* SARAH *enter bg Left and move to door.*

Cut to: cs—WYATT *looking fg.*

CHILDREN: (*os*) (*Crying and shouting.*)

Cut to: mcs—STRANGER *bending down to washbasin* —WYATT *behind Right*—STRANGER *dabs water under his arms*—*he straightens, puts on glasses and steps back to* WYATT.

BILLY and CHILDREN: (*Ad lib yells os.*) Bang, bang.

Cut to: mls—CHILDREN *chasing* BILLY *as they exchange imaginary gunfire*—*cam dollies back and pans Left as* BILLY *runs Left and fg by woman, as* CHILDREN *chase him.*

BILLY and CHILDREN: (*Ad lib imitated yells of gunfire.*) Bang, bang, bang—pow, pow, pow.

BILLY *halts—hold him mcs.*

BILLY: Pow, pow, pow. Ppttwanng. You can't hit me, I'm invisible. I'm invisible.

Mud hits BILLY *on chest.*

CHILDREN: (*Ad lib laughter.*)

*Cut to: mcs—*STRANGER *and* WYATT *standing against building door bearing symbols.*

CHILDREN: (*os*) (*Ad lib laughter.*)

STRANGER *and* WYATT *turn bg, open door and move bg into building, revealing* SARAH *and* LISA *inside—* STRANGER *moves bg behind* SARAH.

STRANGER: Hey, Sarah, how's it—

Cut to: mls—int barn/kitchen area—low angle: SARAH, STRANGER *and* WYATT *standing at table—* LISA *bg Left—another girl Right fg, back to cam, another girl Left.*

STRANGER: —goin"?

Cam dollies back and pans Left as SARAH *crosses Left to shelf and puts down knife—pan Right past others as* SARAH *moves fg down steps, crosses Right to animals and couples on straw platform—*SARAH *bends down to goat.*

SARAH: Hey, Rudolph, what are you eating?

Cut to: mcs—int barn—day—low angle: WYATT *reaches up to wall hanging which reads: L.A.P.D.*

SARAH: (*os*) Thanks for the stuff you brought.

STRANGER: (*os*) Yeah. How's it going?

> *Cut to: mls—girl on upper level getting dressed, back to cam—*WYATT's *hand enters Right fg and picks up butcher knife.*

SARAH: (*os*) We just can't take anymore, Stranger. Just too many people dropping in.

> *Pan Left past* WYATT's *hand and tilt up to opening in roof—walls lined with symbols.*

SARAH: (*os*) Oh, I'm not talking about you and your friends, you know that. (*Sighs.*) And like the week before, Susan—

> *Cut to: mcs—low angle:* WYATT—*he moves Right fg down steps and exits—*LISA *enters Right at head of steps, stops and turns fg to look after* WYATT.

SARAH: (*os*) —dropped in with twelve people from Easter City. She wanted to take ten pounds of rice with her.

STRANGER: (*os*) Yeah.

SARAH: (*os*) Well, naturally—

Cut to: mls—low angle: from WYATT's *pov to steps leading up to loft—cam dollies up and pans from Right to Left holding low angle of sun shining down through opening in roof.*

SARAH: (*os*) —we had to say no.

STRANGER: (*os*) Right.

SARAH: (*os*) So she gets all up tight and she breaks out some hash—and she won't give us any. Oh, and—

Cut to: mls—low angle: WYATT *on steps to loft—pan Left as he moves Left and fingers flag.*

SARAH: (*os*) —that's not all. The next morning they went outside to start their bus and they couldn't get it started.

CHILD: (*os*) No!

STRANGER: (*os*) (*Chuckles.*) Sarah, I bet you haven't—

Cut to: mcs—low angle: LISA.

STRANGER: (*os*) —had anybody around like me to rap to, have you?

*Cut to: ms—*STRANGER *snuggling up to* SARAH—*girl seated bg Left.*

STRANGER: I don't have to tell you how it is, Sarah. You know, I—I love you and I want you to rap—

SARAH: (*Laughs.*)

STRANGER: —Oh, I want you to rap—

SARAH: Cut that out!

STRANGER: Rap, rap—

81

LISA *enters Left and leans on* STRANGER.

LISA: I guess nobody else here is interested, but I would sure like to meet your friend.

STRANGER: I bet you'd like to do more than that.

SARAH: (*Giggles.*)

LISA: I think he's beautiful.

STRANGER: He's beautiful.

BILLY: (*os*) Hey!

> *Cut to: mls—int barn—low angle:* BILLY *in kitchen area.*

BILLY: What is that—uh—weird thing up there on the hill, man? It looks like—

> *Cut to: ms*—LISA, STRANGER *and* SARAH—WYATT *Right moves down ladder to them.*

BILLY: (*os*) —a stage for a light opera company or something.

LISA: That—that's the mime troupe stage. They've gone down to the hot springs to bathe.

> *Cut to: mls—low angle:* BILLY.

BILLY: Mime troupe? (*Laughs and imitates them clumsily.*)

JOANNE: (*os*) Hey, Lisa—

*Cut to: ms—*LISA, STRANGER, SARAH *and* WYATT— JOANNE *bg Left.*

SARAH: Oh!

SARAH *moves fg and exits—*LISA *steps bg to* JOANNE *—*STRANGER *and* WYATT *cross Left and exit—pan Left slightly, revealing little girl seated on tire suspended on rope.*

JOANNE: Wha-what does this mean? "Starting brings misfortune. Per—"

*Cut to: ms—*STRANGER *sits on step Left—*WYATT *moving to Left looking upward—*SARAH *bg holding dog—couples lying bg on bed of hay.*

JOANNE: (*os*) "—serverence brings danger."

BILLY *enters Left as he leaps into scene and poses.*

BILLY: La-la!

JOANNE: (*os*) "Not every—

*Cut to: ms—*JOANNE *seated between boy and* LISA *reads book aloud.*

JOANNE: "—demand for change in the existing order should be heeded."

*Cut to: mls—*BILLY *standing between* WYATT *and* SARAH*—*STRANGER *seated Left—*BILLY *snuggles up to* SARAH*—she pushes him away and pulls his hat down over his eyes—*BILLY *falls back.*

JOANNE: (*os*) "On the other hand, repeated and well-founded complaints should not fail to a hearing."

LISA: (*os*) Well, when one talk—

THE DEVIL: (*os*) Hear ye, hear ye, hear ye!

> *Cut to: ms—*STRANGER—MIME TROUPE *bg at foot of steps.*

THE DEVIL: We've come to play for our dinner—

> SARAH *and* LISA *enter fg and move bg up steps.*

THE DEVIL: Or should I say, stay for our dinner.

> *Cut to: cs—*WYATT *looking to Left.*

THE DEVIL: (*os*) Or even—slay for our dinner.

> *Cam pulls back bringing in* BILLY *beside* WYATT.
>
> *Cut to: ms—*STRANGER—MIME TROUPE *bg in kitchen area—*WOMAN *in Cleopatra headdress moves fg down steps.*

WOMAN: Oh! Men at war. How ghastly, ghastly.

THE DEVIL: Ahhh!

> *Cut to: mcs—*BILLY *and* WYATT *facing Left.*

THE DEVIL: (*os*) We've come to drink your wine. Take your food and take pleasure in your women.

BILLY: (*Laughs.*)

SECOND WOMAN: (*os*) It's fantastic.

> *Cut to: mcs—*WOMAN *in Cleopatra headdress posing Left fg—*THE DEVIL *behind Right seated next to* STRANGER—SECOND WOMAN *behind them—others bg in kitchen area.*

SECOND WOMAN: The water in that river is about eighty degrees. You put your hand in about a foot away, it's below freezing.

*Cut to: mcs—*WYATT *and* BILLY *looking off Left.*

BILLY: (*Chuckles—indistinct, mutters.*) Here, zaba!

BILLY *holds joint to* WYATT, *who takes puff.*

SARAH: (*os*) Now, come on, come on, I've got to get dinner on. Come on.

*Cut to: mls—*SARAH *on steps—*STRANGER *and second girl seated Right—*THE DEVIL *and first* WOMAN *Left fg—others in bg.*

Ad lib groans and mutters.

SARAH: Come on! Out.

THE DEVIL: What is this I hear? Out? Who said out to me?

SARAH *grabs* THE DEVIL *and pulls him bg to stairs.*

THE DEVIL: I—Unhand me! I played—

SARAH: Out, out! Out! Out!

THE DEVIL: (*Overlaps.*) Ye shall hear this. Evil eye on this place. A double whammy for all of you.

*Cut to: mcs—*BILLY *and* WYATT.

WOMAN: (*os*) (*Indistinct.*) —you lay down with dogs you get up with fleas.

THE DEVIL: (*os*) Come, my dear. We won't play here.

WYATT *exits Left followed by* BILLY.

Cut to: mls—STRANGER *and* WYATT *moving up steps to kitchen*—SARAH *Left on steps—three girls in bg fixing meal*—BILLY *enters fg.*

BILLY: Wow, wow, wow!

SARAH: Wow!

SARAH *playfully kicks at* BILLY *as he moves up steps by her.*

BILLY: Wow!

SARAH: (*Laughs.*)

BILLY: A little of that.

SARAH: Cut it out.

SARAH *moves up steps with* BILLY.

BILLY: I like you. (*Laughs.*)

SARAH: (*Laughs.*)

WYATT *and* STRANGER *exit out door*—BILLY *follows.*

Cut to: mls—ext commune—women and children gathered fg—BILLY, WYATT *and* STRANGER *moving bg to rear of barn.*

CHILDREN: (*Ad lib laughter.*)

Cut to: ms—pan Left with man's legs as he walks Left barefoot over bare ground.

STRANGER: (*os*) Uh, you see, what happened here is these

people got here late in the summer. Too late to plant. But the weather was beautiful and—

> *Cut to: ms—pan Left with man, waist down in scene, as he moves Right throwing seeds.*

STRANGER: (*os*) —it was easy livin', and everything was fine. And then came that winter—

> *Cut to: ms—cam dollies Left as* STRANGER, BILLY *and* WYATT *walk to Left.*

STRANGER: —there were forty or fifty of them here living in this one-room place down here. Nothing to eat—starving. Out by the side of the road looking for dead horses.

WYATT: Hmmm.

STRANGER: Anything they could get ahold of. Now there's— there's eighteen or twenty of them left—and—

> *The three stop and look fg—hold them ms.*

STRANGER: —they're city kids. Look at them.

> *Cut to: ms—ext field—boys and girls moving back and forth across field throwing seeds—cam dollies back.*

STRANGER: (*os*) But they're getting this crop in.

> *Cut to: ms—pan Right as two boys walk Right tossing seeds, faces os.*

STRANGER: (*os*) They're gonna stay here until it's harvested. That's the whole thing.

> *Cut to: ms—pan Right along boys and girls sowing seeds.*

Cut to: ms—BILLY, STRANGER *and* WYATT.

WYATT: Uh. You get much rain here, man?

STRANGER: I guess we're gonna have to dance for that.

> *Ad lib laughter.*
>
> *Pan Left as* STRANGER *walks bg Left to two men in field*—WYATT *and* BILLY *cross Left and stop—hold them ms as* BILLY *picks up something from ground.*

BILLY: Look at this, man—sea shells—man, dig. (*Chuckles.*) You dig that?

> JACK *enters Left, pushes* BILLY *aside and moves Right sowing seeds.*

BILLY: This is nothing but sand, man. They ain't gonna make it, man—they ain't gonna grow anything here.

> *Cut to: mcs*—WYATT *looking Right*—STRANGER *and man seated bg on ground*—WYATT *looks to Left.*

WYATT: They're gonna make it. Dig, man.

> *Cut to: mls—shooting from* WYATT's *pov to two girls making scarecrow.*

WYATT: (*os*) They're gonna make it.

> *Cut to: ms*—STRANGER *and two men as they pass pipe among them.*
> *Cut to: ls—two girls in field making scarecrow.*
> *Cut to: mcs—int barn—day*—JACK *standing between* STRANGER *Right and worker Left.*

BABY: (*os*) (*Cries.*)

Cam, on JACK, *pans Left in 360° camera move of entire circle of people, including* BILLY, WYATT, SARAH, LISA, MIME TROUPE *and workers—cam stops on return to* JACK *and holds mcs of* JACK *between* STRANGER *and worker.*

JACK: We've planted our seeds. We ask that our efforts be worthy to produce simple food for our simple taste. We ask that our efforts be rewarded. And we thank you for the food we eat from other hands—

BABY: (*os*) (*Gurgles.*)

JACK: —that we may share it with our fellow man and be even more generous when it is from our own. Thank you for a place to make a stand.

GROUP: (*os*) (*In unison.*) Amen.

CHILD: (*os*) Amen.

JACK: Let's eat.

*Cut to: ms—ext commune—day—*BILLY *standing—
people seated about on ground—*LISA *and* WYATT *bg.*

MIME TROUPE: (*os*) (*Ad lib.*) Ahhh, hark ye, generals. Hark
ye all. Time has come for curtain call.

Pan Right past BILLY *and others as* WYATT *and* LISA
*move forward Right to tent—hold them ms as she
reaches into tent and brings out skins—they turn and
head bg toward rock.*

MIME TROUPE: (*os*) (*Singing.*)
"How do you wear your hair"—

*Cut to: ms—*BILLY *in midst of people looking off
Right.*

Ad lib indistinct chatter.

MIME TROUPE: (*os*) (*Singing.*)
"—Does your hair hang low?
Do you tie it in a ribbon?

Do you tie it in a bow?
Do you wear it over your shoulder
  Like a Continental soldier—"

Pan up Left as BILLY *rises, bringing in* MIME TROUPE *bg on stage.*

MIME TROUPE:
  "—Does your hair hang low?
Oh, does your hair hang low—"

*Cut to: mls—*LISA *and* WYATT *at rock—they sit on skins—group Left fg.*

MIME TROUPE: (*os*) (*Singing.*)
  "—Do you tie it in a ribbon?
Do you wear it over your shoulder—"

Cut to: ms—low angle: LISA *and* WYATT *settling down on ground.*

MIME TROUPE: (*os*) (*Singing.*)
  "—Like a Continental soldier

95

Does your hair hang low?

Repeat above lyrics over following dialogue.

LISA: Are you an Aquarius?

WYATT *shakes his head.*

LISA: Pisces?

WYATT: (*Snickers.*) Hmm-mmm.

LISA: I guessed right. Do you like our place here?

WYATT: Yeah.

> *Cut to: mls—*SARAH *standing by stage—*MIME TROUPE *on stage, singing.*
>
> *Pan Left past* TROUPE *as* SARAH *strolls to Left, enters to* BILLY *and pauses.*
>
> *Singing continues os.*
>
> *Cut to: ms—shooting from behind* STRANGER *to* SARAH *approaching—*BILLY *in bg—*MIME TROUPE *and others bg—*STRANGER *turns fg putting arm around* SARAH.
>
> *Indistinct singing in bg.*
>
> *Cut to: mls—*STRANGER *and* SARAH *join group behind tent Left—boy Right fg in front of tent stoops down.*
>
> *Indistinct singing os.*
>
> *Cut to: ms—*BILLY *looking Left.*
>
> *Indistinct singing and crowd noise os.*
>
> *Pan Left as* BILLY *walks to Left and enters to* STRANGER, SARAH *and group—*BILLY *makes to join*

them—boy Right rises and holds cross out in front of
BILLY—*he stops*—STRANGER *moves fg to* BILLY.

STRANGER: Who sent ya?

> BILLY *turns fg—pan Right past* STRANGER *and group*
> *as* BILLY *crosses Right and enters in front of* MIME
> TROUPE—*they paw at him.*

MIME TROUPE: (*Singing.*)
  "Does your hair hang low?
  Do you tie it in a ribbon?
  Do you tie it in a bow?
  Do you wear it over your shoulder
    like a Continental soldier?"

> *Pan Right past group as* BILLY *pulls away and moves*
> *bg Right, bringing in* LISA *and* WYATT *seated alone*
> *against rock—hold mls as he joins them.*

Cut to: ms—low angle: shooting between BILLY's *legs to* LISA *and* WYATT—BILLY *stumbles bg and falls against rock.*

BILLY: (*Gasps.*) Whew. Man, look, I gotta get of here, man. Now we—we got things we want to do, man, like—I just—uh—I gotta get out of here, man.

LISA: Hey, hmmmm—could you take me and—and my friend —uh—over across the canyon?

WYATT: Yeah—anything.

LISA: Hey, it—it won't be out of your way—honest.

WYATT: It's all right. It's all right.

LISA hands joint to WYATT, rises and exits Left fg—WYATT hands joint to BILLY.

BILLY: Hey, man, we're not no travelin' bureau, man. Why don't they get their own ride in?

WYATT: Hey, hey, hey. We're eating their food.

BILLY: (*Sighs.*) All right, man.

BILLY drags on joint and hands it to WYATT.

BILLY: Get 'em together though, man.

WYATT: Right.

WYATT rises and exits Left—BILLY settles down on ground.

BILLY: (*Gasps.*)

Cut to: mls—ext commune—day—shooting from be-

hind hippies to MIMES *on stage*—JACK *doing mime dance*—STRANGER *and* SARAH *walk bg through scene.*

Ad lib chatter and laughter.

Cut to: cs—JOANNE *holding onto her own leg and laughing*—*child beside her.*

Ad lib chatter and laughter.

Cut to: ms—JACK *doing mime dance, back to cam.*

Ad lib chatter and laughter.

Cut to: mcs—JACK *doing mime dance, back to cam* —*he turns fg.*

Ad lib chatter and laughter.

Cut to: ls—*ext valley/stream*—*day*—WYATT, LISA, SARAH *and* BILLY *walking single file bg along bank of stream.*

Music over—"Wasn't Born to Follow."

Cut to: ms—*pan Right as* SARAH *and* BILLY *walk to Right*—*cam zooms back and pans Right past them to* WYATT *and* LISA *walking to Right*—SARAH *and* BILLY *enter Left.*

Cut to: ms—ext grotto—day—high angle: rippling water SARAH *enters swimming nude in water, followed by* BILLY *and* LISA.

Cut to: ls—high angle: river—pan down bringing in SARAH, LISA *and* BILLY *in grotto—*WYATT *seated Left on wall.*

Cut to: ms—low angle: WYATT *seated on wall.*

Cut to: mls—high angle: SARAH, LISA *and* BILLY *in water—*WYATT *partially seen Left seated on wall.*

*Cut to: mcs—*LISA *swimming fg—*BILLY *and* SARAH *in bg.*

Cut to: ms—low angle: WYATT.

Cut to: ms—high angle: LISA *holding onto* WYATT*'s legs—she turns bg.*

*Cut to: mls—*SARAH *and* BILLY *in water—*LISA*'s legs in fg kicking.*

Cut to: ms—low angle: WYATT.

Cut to: ms—high angle: SARAH *and* BILLY *playing in water—they submerge.*

Cut to: ms—high angle: from WYATT*'s pov to* LISA *holding onto his legs.*

Cut to: ms—high angle: BILLY *and* SARAH *playing in water.*

*Cut to: ms—*WYATT *in water.*

*Cut to: ms—*LISA *and* BILLY *swimming fg splashing water as water splashes in from fg—*SARAH *in bg.*

*Cut to: ms—*WYATT *splashing water.*

*Cut to: ms—*LISA, BILLY *and* SARAH *swim bg as water enters fg and splashes them.*

*Cut to: mcs—*WYATT *facing Left and splashing water.*

*Cut to: mls—*LISA, BILLY *and* SARAH *swim to wall.*

Cut to: mcs—high angle: WYATT *shakes his head and turns Left.*

Cut to: mcs—high angle: WYATT—*he swims fg and exits under overhanging rock.*

Cut to: ms—ext field—day—pan Right over weeds blowing in breeze, bringing in WYATT, *dressed, standing in field, hand outstretched to weeds—pan up to him and hold mcs.*

*Cut to: mls—*WYATT *looking off Left—valley bg below—*WYATT *turns, walks Right fg and exits.*

*Cut to: cs—ext commune—day—*STRANGER *seated on ground—tent behind him—he holds small object in his hand.*

STRANGER: When you get to the right place, with the right people—

Pan Right bringing WYATT *beside him.*

STRANGER: —quarter this.

WYATT *takes object.*

STRANGER: You know, this could be the right place. The time's running out.

BILLY: *(os)* Hey, man! Hey!

*Cut to: mcs—*BILLY.

BILLY: If we're goin', we're going. Let's go.

*Cut to: mcs—*WYATT *and* STRANGER—STRANGER *holds up his hand to* BILLY *for silence—*WYATT *and* STRANGER *lean back against wall—hold mcs.*

WYATT: Yeah, I'm—I'm hip about time. But I just gotta go.

Cut to: ms—ext Las Vegas, N.M.—main street—day—tuba player marches fg—pan Left with him.

Cut to: mcs—high angle: pan Right with boy playing drum.

Cut to: ms—brass section marching fg.

Cut to: ms—pan down to majorette's legs as she marches to Left—townspeople gathered bg along sidewalk—pan up Left as majorette marches bg.

Cut to: mcs—boy marches Right fg playing instrument.

*Cut to: mls—town school band marches fg playing—*WYATT *in center of them wheeling his bike—he moves fg.*

Cut to: mcs—pan Left as WYATT *wheels Left on cycle.*

Cut to: ms—pan Left as BILLY *wheels cycle Left fg.*

Cut to: ms—tracking in behind WYATT *wheeling bg with band—pan Left past him to* BILLY.

Cut to: mcs—pan Left with girl playing piccolo.

*Cut to: mcs—*WYATT *wheeling Left—rope twirls around him—pan up Right past* WYATT *to cowboy on horse.*

Cut to: mcs—pan Left as boy marches Left fg playing trombone—track in behind him as he marches bg.

Cut to: ms—shooting from behind BILLY *Left fg to* WYATT *bg Right wheeling cycle bg.*

Cut to: ls—majorettes approaching, followed by band.

Cut to: ms—low angle: WYATT *moves fg in center of band.*

Cut to: cus—revolving red light on roof of police car.

Cut to: mls—band marching Left with WYATT *and*

*BILLY in their midst—police car Right following—
pan Left as band turns off bg onto side street and
BILLY and WYATT wheel Left and exit, followed by
police car.*

*Cut to: mcs—int cell block—day—BILLY in cell
looking fg—WYATT behind Left, back to cam—steel
door closes fg.*

BILLY: Parading without a permit? You gotta be kidding. I
mean, you know who this is, man? This is Captain America.
I'm Billy. Hey, we're headliners, baby. We played every fair
in this part of the country. I mean, for top dollar, too.

BILLY turns bg.

BILLY: *(Sighs.)* Oh, man.

*Cut to: insert: int cell—day—symbol on wall with
lettering: I Love God.*

Cut to: mcs—cam pans along wall bearing drawings.

*Cut to: insert: flash shots of drawings on cell walls—
stop and hold mcs of plaque on wall reading: Jesus
Christ the same yesterday to-day and forever.*

BILLY: *(os) (Sighs.)* Weirdo hicks, man. A bunch of weirdo
hicks, you know. Huh. Parading without a permit, man!

*Cut to: ms—int cell—day—high angle: WYATT
asleep on bunk.*

BILLY: *(os) (Sighs.)*

Cut to: ms—int cell—BILLY seated on bunk.

BILLY: *(Sighs.)*

*He rises—cam dollies back as he moves fg, running
his fingers through his hair—he stops in doorway to
adjoining cell—cam continues to dolly back bringing
in* GEORGE *Right on cot wrestling about.*

GEORGE: *(Moans.)* Oh, no—

Cut to: ms—high angle: GEORGE *waking.*

GEORGE: —what did I do now? *(Moans.)*

GEORGE *sits up and faces Left.*

GEORGE: Oh, what am I gonna do now? Mmmm. Mmmmm—my head.

Pan up as GEORGE, *holding onto wall, rises.*

GEORGE: *(Groans.)* All right now, George—what are you gonna do now? I mean, you promised these people now. You promised these people—and you promised these people and—

GEORGE *faces Left and leans on cell door—door swings shut.*

Cut to: ms—high angle: WYATT *asleep—he wakes as cell door Right clangs shut.*

GEORGE: *(os) (Indistinct.)* —They're not gonna believe you, George.

*Cut to: mls—*WYATT *on cot Left—*GEORGE *standing Right holding onto cell door—*BILLY *on other side of door—he pushes it open and* GEORGE *staggers back.*

BILLY: *(Yells.)* Hey, man, would you mind—

Cut to: cs—shooting through cell door to BILLY.

BILLY: —you just woke my friend up.

GEORGE: *(os)* Oh, yeah, well I—I—

Cut to: cs—shooting through cell door to GEORGE.

GEORGE: —I'm—uh—I'm real sorry. I didn't realize I—uh—I didn't realize—

Cut to: cs—shooting through cell door at BILLY.
Cut to: cs—shooting through cell door at GEORGE.

GEORGE: *(Sighs.)* My head—

BILLY: *(os)* Hey, man, if—

> *Cut to: cs—shooting through cell door at* BILLY.

BILLY: —you don't shut your mouth, man—you ain't gonna have a head.

> *Cut to: cs—shooting through cell door at* GEORGE.

GEORGE: *(Yawns.)*

> GUARD *enters bg at other cell door.*
>
> *Cut to: cs—shooting through cell door at* BILLY *staring fg.*
>
> *Cut to: cs—shooting through cell door at* GEORGE— GUARD *in bg.*

GUARD: See you're up, Mister Hanson. You'll feel a lot better after this.

GEORGE *looks bg to* GUARD.

GEORGE: Oh—

> *Cut to: ms—*BILLY *in doorway between cells—* GEORGE *standing Right—*WYATT *lying Left on cot.*

GEORGE: Oh. Thank you, Bob.

> WYATT *sits up as* GEORGE *exits Right fg.*

GEORGE: *(os)* I guess I—

> *Cut to: ms—*GEORGE *moves to* GUARD *holding cup and aspirins.*

GEORGE: —I guess I really tied one on last night. I must've had a helluva good time.

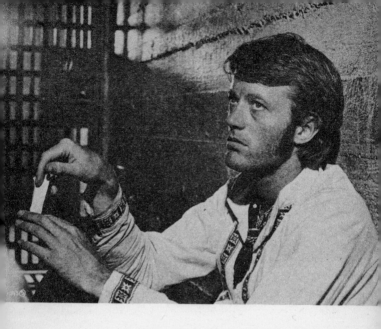

Cut to: ms—WYATT *rises*—BILLY *in doorway.*

GEORGE: *(os)* I wish I could remember it.

    Cut to: ms—GEORGE *and* GUARD—BILLY *enters fg
and joins them.*

BILLY: Hey, man—uh—you don't—you don't think you could
get me a cigarette, do you?

GUARD: You animals ain't smart enough to play with fire.

GEORGE: Oh, no, no, no. That's all right, Bob, that's all right.
They're good boys. You can give 'em a cigarette.

    GUARD *takes out pack of cigarettes and holds them
out to* BILLY—BILLY *takes one.*

BILLY: Thanks, Mister. You got a match?

GUARD: Yeah.

> GUARD *hands matches to* BILLY, *turns and moves out of cell into corridor.*

BILLY: *(Sighs.)*

GEORGE: Thank you, Bob.

> *Pan Left past* GUARD *as* GEORGE *and* BILLY *move Left and enter to* WYATT *seated against wall.*

BILLY: *(Coughs.)* Listen, I'm—uh—you know, I'm sorry about —uh—you know, the misunderstanding, you know.

GEORGE: Oh, that's all right. There's no misunderstanding— we're all in the same cage here.

> *Hold the three ms as* BILLY *and* GEORGE *sit on cot Left of* WYATT.

GEORGE: Oh.

BILLY: You must be some important dude, man. Like, you know, that treatment.

GEORGE: A dude? *(Looking at* WYATT.*)* What does he mean, "dude"? Dude ranch?

BILLY: A dude. *(Laughs.)*

WYATT: No, no.

> *Cut to: cs—*WYATT.

WYATT: Dude means—uh—a nice guy, you know. Dude means a regular sort of person.

> *Cut to: mcs—*GEORGE—BILLY *behind Left.*

GEORGE: Well, you boys don't look like you're from this part of the country. You're lucky I'm here to see that you don't get into anything.

Cut to: cs—WYATT.

WYATT: Anything?

Cut to: mcs—GEORGE—BILLY behind Left.

GEORGE: Well, they got this here—see—uh—scissor-happy "Beautify America" thing goin' on around here. They're tryin' to make everybody look like Yul Brynner.

Cut to: cs—WYATT.

GEORGE: *(os)* They used—uh—rusty razor blades on the—

Cut to: mcs—GEORGE—BILLY behind Left.

GEORGE: —last two long-hairs that they brought in here—

BILLY: *(Sighs.)*

GEORGE: —and I wasn't here to protect them. You see—uh— I'm—uh—I'm a lawyer.

> GEORGE *reaches bg to suit jacket behind* BILLY *and takes out card from pocket—he hands card to* BILLY.

GEORGE: Done a lot of work for the A.C.L.U.

BILLY: "George Hanson."

> BILLY *hands card Right to* WYATT *os.*
> *Cut to: cs—WYATT looks at card.*

BILLY: *(os)* Listen, you think you can help us get out of here with no sweat?

> *Cut to: cs*—GEORGE.

GEORGE: Oh, I imagine that I can, if you haven't killed anybody. Least nobody white.

> *Cut to: ms*—*int jail office*—*day*—WYATT *and* GEORGE *at counter*—BILLY *behind*—SHERIFF *and* GUARD *bg Right behind counter.*

GEORGE: You see—there—twenty-five dollars. Not too bad. No razor blades. You know what I mean.

WYATT: Very groovy, George. Thank you.

GEORGE: Very groovy. Very groovy. *(To guards.)* See there. I bet nobody ever said that to you. Oh, by the way, Bob—

Cut to: mcs—GEORGE *facing Right*—BILLY *and* WYATT *behind him.*

GEORGE: —thanks for the aspirin before.

SHERIFF: *(os)* George, I'm gettin' to—I'm getting to think you're a regular regular around here. I'm not going to tell your dad.

Cut to: ms—*shooting from behind* GEORGE *to* GUARD *and* SHERIFF.

SHERIFF: I don't know, George, you just got to be more careful.

GEORGE: Yeah, well Pat—uh—that'd be real good if the—uh—

> GEORGE *puts money on counter by* SHERIFF's *hand.*
>
> *Cut to: mcs—*GEORGE *with back to camera facing* BILLY *and* WYATT *behind.*

GEORGE: —powers that be wouldn't hear about this. I mean, the old man hasn't been feeling too good. You know what I mean?

SHERIFF: *(os)* Well, now George, you know we won't tell your dad about that.

> *Cut to: ms—shooting from behind* GEORGE *to* SHERIFF *and* GUARD.

SHERIFF: That right, Bob?

GUARD: Right.

> *Cut to: mcs—*GEORGE—WYATT *and* BILLY *behind.*

GEORGE: Well—what d'you say we—uh—take a look at these super machines we've been hearing so much about.

BILLY: Let's get it on.

> *Cut to: mcs—*GEORGE—*he turns bg to* GUARD *and* SHERIFF.

GEORGE: Thanks a lot, Bob.

SHERIFF: Oh.

GEORGE: See you later.

> GEORGE *turns and exits Left fg.*

> *Cut to: ls—ext Las Vegas, N.M.—day—shooting across street to front of police station—firehouse to Left with* BILLY, POLICEMAN *and* WYATT *in doorway—*BILLY *and* WYATT *on motorcycles—*GEORGE *emerges from police station.*

GEORGE: *(Talking to someone os inside jail.)* I'll take care of it later. Don't worry about it. Good-bye.

> GEORGE *walks along sidewalk to* POLICEMAN *with* WYATT *and* BILLY.

GEORGE: All right, Carl.

Cut to: ms—ext firehouse—shooting from behind BILLY *standing Left of motorcycle to* GEORGE *handing money to* POLICEMAN.

GEORGE: Thanks a million. Say hello to the missus for me, will ya?

POLICEMAN: Yes, sir.

GEORGE: All right.

> POLICEMAN *moves to Left and exits—*GEORGE *takes out pint of whisky.*

GEORGE: Here's to the first of the day, fellas.

> *Cut to: cs—ext sidewalk—*WYATT *looking fg smiling.*
>
> *Cut to: mcs—*GEORGE *raises bottle in toast.*

GEORGE: To ol' D. H. Lawrence.

> GEORGE *drinks from bottle.*

GEORGE: *(Gasps—makes noise, slaps elbow.)* Nik, nik, nik, nik, nik—Indians! Whew!

> GEORGE *steps fg and holds bottle os.*
>
> *Cut to: cs—*BILLY *takes drink from bottle and hands it fg os.*

BILLY: *(Gasps.)*

> *Cut to: cs—*GEORGE *turns to face Right.*

·GEORGE: You know, I must've started off to Mardi Gras six or seven times. Never got further than the state line.

*Cut to: ms—*GEORGE *and* WYATT—GEORGE *takes out wallet.*

GEORGE: The Governor of Louisiana give me this.

GEORGE *takes out card from wallet.*

GEORGE: "Madame Tinkertoy's House of Blue Lights. Corner of Bourbon and Toulouse, New Orleans, Louisiana." Now this is supposed to be the finest whorehouse in the South.

*Cut to: cs—*WYATT.

GEORGE: *(os)* These ain't no—

*Cut to: cs—*GEORGE *facing Right.*

GEORGE: —pork chops. These are U.S. Prime.

*Cut to: cs—*BILLY.

BILLY: Out a site, man.

*Cut to: ms—*GEORGE *and* WYATT—GEORGE *puts card back in wallet.*

GEORGE: Oh, I'd like to get over there. Ha. How long—uh—how long did you boys say it was gonna take you to get down there?

WYATT: Oh, about two or three days.

GEORGE: Two or three days—is that right? Oh, boy—I sure wish I was goin' with ya.

WYATT: Oh, yeah? You got a helmet?

*Cut to: cs—*GEORGE.

GEORGE: Oh. Oh, I've got a helmet. *(Laughs.)* Oh, I got a beauty.

> *Cut to: ms—ext highway—day—*WYATT *and* GEORGE
> *riding double on motorcycle—*GEORGE *wearing gold
> football helmet—he laughs and waves—cam trucks
> Right with them, bringing in* BILLY *bg alongside.*

> *Music over—*"If You Want To Be a Bird."

> *Cut to: ms—ext highway—cam trucks back Right as*
> BILLY, WYATT *and* GEORGE *ride to Right—zoom in
> past* BILLY *to mcs of* WYATT *and* GEORGE*—cam pulls
> back to ms bringing in* BILLY*—pan down from the
> three to wheels of cycles.*

> *Cut to: ms—cam trucks back Right holding on mo-
> torcycle—pan up to* BILLY.

> *Cut to: ms—cam trucks Right with* WYATT *and*
> GEORGE*—*BILLY *bg on other side—*BILLY *stands up.*

Cut to: mls—cam trucks back as BILLY, WYATT *and* GEORGE *ride fg—*BILLY *standing up—*GEORGE *stretches out his arms.*

Cut to: mls—cam trucks in behind BILLY *standing up in seat—he sits down.*

Cut to: mls—cam trucks in behind BILLY, GEORGE *and* WYATT *riding bg—they wave to man in field.*

Cut to: mcs—cam trucks Left with WYATT—*pan Right bringing in* GEORGE.

Cut to: ms—cam trucks Left with WYATT *and* GEORGE—BILLY *bg alongside.*

*Cut to: ls—*WYATT, GEORGE *and* BILLY *riding bg.*

Cut to: ms—cam trucks Left with WYATT *and* GEORGE *riding Left—*BILLY *bg alongside.*

Cut to: mls—cam trucks in behind BILLY, GEORGE *and* WYATT *riding bg—*BILLY *and* GEORGE *flap their arms.*

Cut to: mls—cam trucks back as BILLY, WYATT *and* GEORGE *ride fg—*GEORGE *sitting up flapping his arms.*

Cut to: mls—cam trucks in behind BILLY, GEORGE *and* WYATT *as they ride bg.*

Cut to: mls—cam trucks Left across bridge, holding on dried riverbed bg.

Cut to: mls—cam trucks back Left as WYATT, GEORGE *and* BILLY *ride Left across bridge.*

Cut to: ls—cam trucks Left holding on cowhands herding sheep through dried riverbed.

Cut to: mls—cam trucks back as GEORGE, WYATT *and* BILLY *ride Left—they pull ahead and exit Left.*

Cut to: mls—cam trucks back as BILLY, WYATT *and* GEORGE *travel fg.*

Cut to: ls—cam trucks in behind WYATT, GEORGE *and* BILLY *riding bg.*

Cut to: mls—ext road—night—pan Left as GEORGE, BILLY *and* WYATT *ride Left bg off road and stop under trees.*

Cut to: els—ext campsite—night—low angle: moon in sky—pan down to cs of GEORGE *seated on ground staring fg at helmet in his hands.*

BILLY: *(os) (Laughs—ad lib mutters.)*

*Cut to: mls—*BILLY *seated on ground between motor-cycles—he claps his hands.*

GEORGE: *(os)* Well, ol' buddy.

*Cut to: ms—*GEORGE *holding helmet—cam dollies back slowly, bringing in* WYATT *seated Right on ground as* GEORGE *talks.*

GEORGE: I never thought I'd ever see you again. You know, I threw this thing away one week ago. My mother, of all people, retrieved it. I can't understand that.

Cam stops and holds the two mls.

GEORGE: She didn't even want me to play football. Always afraid I was gonna get hurt. And here, twelve years later, I find it on my pillow with a note pinned next to it saying: "Save this for your son."

GEORGE *raises bottle in toast.*

*Cut to: mls—*BILLY.

BILLY: *(Laughs.)*

*Cut to: ms—*GEORGE *drinks from bottle—he flaps his arms.*

GEORGE: Nik, nik, nik, nik—Fire!

*Cut to: ms—*WYATT *rolling joint—he holds it out Left.*

WYATT: Do this instead.

> *Cut to: ms—GEORGE—WYATT's hand in Right holding joint.*

GEORGE: Oh, no thanks. I got some—uh—store-bought right over here of my own.

> *Cut to: ms—WYATT.*

WYATT: No, man—this is grass.

> *Cut to: mcs—GEORGE looking fg to WYATT's hand holding joint.*

GEORGE: You—you mean marijuana?

> *Cut to: mcs—WYATT.*

WYATT: Yeah.

> *Cut to: mcs—GEORGE—WYATT's hand in fg holding joint.*

GEORGE: Lord have mercy. Is that what that is?

> *Cut to: ms—WYATT holding joint out Left.*

> *Cut to: ms—GEORGE looking at joint held in WYATT's hand Right—GEORGE takes joint and WYATT's hand withdraws.*

GEORGE: Well, let me see that.

> *Cut to: mcs—GEORGE looking at joint—he sniffs at it.*

GEORGE: Mmmm-mmm. Mmmm.

*Cut to: ms—*WYATT.

WYATT: Go ahead, George—light it up.

*Cut to: mcs—*GEORGE.

GEORGE: Oh, no, no, no, no. I—I—I couldn't do that. I mean, I've got enough problems with the—the booze and all. I mean I—I can't afford to get hooked.

*Cut to: mcs—*WYATT *rolling another joint.*

WYATT: Oh, no—you won't get hooked.

*Cut to: mcs—*GEORGE.

GEORGE: Yeah, well, I know, but I mean, it—it—it leads to harder stuff.

*Cut to: mcs—*WYATT.

*Cut to: ms—*GEORGE.

GEORGE: Is that—uh—you—you—you—you say it's all right?

*Cut to: mcs—*WYATT *smiles and looks down.*

*Cut to: mcs—*GEORGE.

GEORGE: Well—uh—all right then—uh—how—how do I do it?

GEORGE *leans Right fg.*

*Cut to: mcs—*WYATT.

WYATT: Here.

He lights match.

*Cut to: mcs—*GEORGE—WYATT's *hands in fg holding lighted match—*GEORGE *leans down to light up joint; match goes out.*

WYATT: *(os)* Oh, wait a second.

WYATT's *hands withdraw and re-enter with lighted match.*

*Cut to: mcs—*WYATT *holding lighted match Left fg—* GEORGE's *head in Left fg as he lights up joint.*

*Cut to: mcs—*GEORGE *leans back and takes drag.*

*Cut to: mcs—*WYATT *looks Left fg.*

*Cut to: mcs—*GEORGE.

GEORGE: Well—uh—that's—that's got a real nice—uh—taste to it. Though I don't suppose it'll do me much good, though. I mean, I'm so used to the booze and everything.

*Cut to: mcs—*WYATT.

WYATT: You gotta hold it in your lungs longer, George.

GEORGE: *(os)* Oh.

> *Cut to: mcs—GEORGE takes big drag, holds it and looks off Left.*

BILLY: *(os)* Oh, wow!

> *Cut to: mcs—BILLY looking up Left fg.*

BILLY: What? What is that, man? Wha-what the hell was that, man?

> *Cut to: mcs—WYATT rolling joint—he looks up fg.*

WYATT: Huh?

> *Cut to: mcs—BILLY.*

BILLY: No, man. Like, hey, man. Wow! I was watching this object, man—like—like the satellite that we saw the other night—right? And like it was just going right across the sky, man. And then, I mean, it just suddenly—uh—*(laughs)* it just changed direction and went—uh—whizzing right off, man.

> *Cut to: mcs—WYATT looks skyward.*

BILLY: *(os)* *(Laughs.)* It flashed and—

WYATT: You're stoned out of your mind, man.

> *Cut to: mcs—BILLY.*

BILLY: Oh, yeah, man—like I'm stoned, you know, man. But —like, you know, I saw a satellite, man.

*Cut to: ms—*GEORGE *looking Left.*

BILLY: *(os)* And it was going across the sky—and it flashed three times at me—

*Cut to: mcs—*BILLY.

BILLY: —and zigzagged and whizzed off, man.

*Cut to: mcs—*GEORGE.

BILLY: *(os)* And I saw it.

GEORGE: *(Exhales.)* That was a UFO, beamin' back at ya. Me and Eric Heisman was down in Mexico two weeks ago—we seen forty of 'em flying in formation. They—they—they've got bases all over the world now, you know.

*Cut to: mcs—*WYATT *smoking.*

GEORGE: *(os)* They've been coming here ever since nineteen forty-six—when the scientists first started bouncing radar beams off the moon.

*Cut to: mcs—*GEORGE.

GEORGE: And they have been livin' and workin' among us in vast quantities ever since. The government knows all about 'em.

*Cut to: mls—*BILLY.

BILLY: What are you talkin', man?

*Cut to: ms—*GEORGE.

GEORGE: Mmmm—well, you just seen one of 'em, didn't ya?

*Cut to: mls—*BILLY.

BILLY: Hey, man, I saw a something, man, but I didn't see it workin' here. You know what I mean?

*Cut to: mcs—*GEORGE.

GEORGE: Well, they are people, just like us—from within our own solar system. Except that their society is more highly evolved. I mean, they don't have no wars, they got no monetary system, they don't have any leaders, because, I mean, each man is a leader. I mean, each man—because of their technology, they are able to feed, clothe, house and transport themselves equally—and with no effort.

*Cut to: mcs—*WYATT *staring Right fg.*

WYATT: Wow!

*Cut to: mcs—*BILLY.

BILLY: Well, you know something, man? I think—you want to know what I think?

Cam pans up as BILLY *rises—stops and holds him mcs low angle.*

BILLY: I think this is a crackpot idea. (*Laughs.*) That's what I think. How about that. (*Laughs.*) How about a little of that. Think it's a crackpot idea. I mean, if they're so—

*Cut to: mcs—*GEORGE *staring Left fg.*

BILLY: (*os*) —smart, why don't they just reveal themselves to us, huh—and get it over with? (*Laughs.*)

GEORGE: Why don't they reveal themselves to us is because if they did it would cause a general panic. Now, I mean, we still have leaders—

> *Cut to: mcs—*WYATT *looking skyward.*

GEORGE: *(os)* —upon whom we rely for the release of this information.

> *Cut to: mcs—*GEORGE.

GEORGE: These leaders have decided to repress this information because of the tremendous shock that it would cause to our antiquated systems. Now, the result of this has been that the Venutians have contacted people in all walks of life—all walks of life—*(Laughs.)*

> *Cut to: mcs—*WYATT.

GEORGE: *(os) (Laughs.)* Yes.

> *Cut to: mcs—low angle:* BILLY *standing—pan down as* BILLY *sits on ground—stop and hold him mcs.*

BILLY: *(Sighs.)*

> *Cut to: mcs—*GEORGE *seated facing Left.*
> *Cut to: mcs—*BILLY *settles on ground.*
> *Cut to: mcs—*GEORGE *facing Left fg.*

GEORGE: It—it—it would be a devastating blow to our antiquated systems—so now the Venutians are meeting with people in all walks of life—in an advisory capacity.

> *Cut to: mcs—*BILLY.

GEORGE: *(os)* For once man will have a god-like control—

> *Cut to: mcs—*GEORGE.

GEORGE: —over his own destiny. He will have a chance to transcend and to evolve with some equality for all.

> *Cut to: mcs—*BILLY *looks skyward and motions with his hands.*
>
> *Cut to: mcs—*GEORGE *looks to Right smiling.*
>
> *Cut to: mcs—*WYATT *looking Left fg, smiles.*

WYATT: How's your joint, George?

*Cut to: mcs—*GEORGE *looking to Right.*

GEORGE: Oh, my—I believe—I believe it went out. I got—I got to talkin' so much I clean forgot about—uh—it went out.

*Cut to: mcs—*WYATT.

WYATT: Well, save it—and we'll do it tomorrow morning first thing, right. It gives you a whole new way of looking at the day.

*Cut to: mcs—*GEORGE.

GEORGE: Well, I sure could use that. (*Laughs.*) I sure could use a little of that.

> *Cut to: mls—ext highway—day—*WYATT, GEORGE *and* BILLY *standing at side of highway, backs to cam —*BILLY *moves to motorcycle.*
>
> *Music over—*"Don't Bogart Me."
>
> *Cut to: mcs—ext highway—high angle: cam trucks back holding on motorcycle tire—cam pans up bringing in* BILLY, WYATT *and* GEORGE—*hold them ms traveling fg.*
>
> *Cut to: ms—cam trucks back Right as* BILLY *rides Right fg—*WYATT *and* GEORGE *pull in Left—cam moves in to mcs.*
>
> *Cut to: ls—cam trucks Right along road past cattle grazing in field and two children riding double on horse—they wave.*
>
> *Cut to: ls—cam trucks Left and pans Right holding on horses at side of highway.*
>
> *Cut to: els—cam trucks Left and zooms back, panning Right to two horses galloping across field—pan Left to highway.*

Cut to: mls—low angle: steel girders as cam trucks in.

Cut to: mls—ext highway—day—cam trucks back and pans Left with WYATT, GEORGE *and* BILLY *riding Left—cemetery in bg.*

Cut to: mls—cam trucks in and pans Right holding on building—sign on building reads: Post Office.

Cut to: mls—ext tree-lined street—cam trucks back as WYATT, GEORGE *and* BILLY *ride fg.*

Cut to: ls—cam trucks Left and pans Right holding on plantation house.

Cut to: mls—low angle: trees, as cam trucks in.

Cut to: ls—cam trucks in holding on large building Right—cars parked in parking area.

Cut to: mls—ext Southern town—day—cam trucks back as WYATT, GEORGE *and* BILLY *ride fg.*

Cut to: mls—cam trucks down main street—pans Right to front of store.

Cut to: mls—cam trucks back as GEORGE, WYATT *and* BILLY *ride fg.*

Cut to: ls—cam trucks Left holding on cemetery Right.

*Cut to: ls—ext highway—*WYATT, GEORGE *and* BILLY *parked off highway—pull back and pan Right as they ride onto highway and bg.*

Music segues into "If Six Was Nine."

Cut to: ls—cam trucks Right along road and pans Left holding on Negro section.

Cut to: ls—cam trucks Left along road past shack.

Cut to: mls—low angle: trees, with moss hanging from them—pan Right holding on trees.

Cut to: ms—cam trucks Right as WYATT, GEORGE *and* BILLY *ride bg Right—shacks bg alongside road.*

Cut to: mls—cam trucks Right and pans Left holding on Negro family beside wagon.

Cut to: mls—cam trucks in Left and pans Right holding on shacks alongside highway.

130

Cut to: mls—cam trucks in Right and swift-pans Right along highway.

Cut to: ls—ext Southern town—day—pan Right as WYATT, GEORGE *and* BILLY *approach on highway and turn off Right to restaurant—they park bikes in front and get off—*GEORGE *takes off jacket as the three move to door.*

Music over—"Let's Turkey Trot."

*Cut to: ms—int restaurant—*BILLY, WYATT *and* GEORGE *enter through door.*

*Cut to: mcs—int restaurant—*MAN *seated Right in booth—two more seated Left—reflections of* BILLY, WYATT *and* GEORGE *in mirror on wall—*MEN *look fg —cam dollies back and pans Left past* MEN *in booth and reflections, bringing in* DEPUTY *seated in next booth—stop and hold him mcs.*

DEPUTY: What the hell is this? Troublemakers?

*Cut to: mls—*BILLY, WYATT *and* GEORGE *moving forward to table.*

CAT MAN: (*os*). You name it—

Cut to: mcs—low angle: MAN *seated Left in booth—* DEPUTY *seated across Right—*DEPUTY's *reflection in mirror.*

CAT MAN: —and I'll throw rocks at it, Sheriff.

Cam dollies back.

GIRL #1: (*os*) Ya'all check what just walked in?

Cam pans Left bringing in three GIRLS *seated in booth—reveal* BILLY, GEORGE *and* WYATT *reflected in mirror as they sit down at table.*

GIRL #1: Oh, I like the one in the red shirt with the suspenders.

GIRL #2: Mmm-mmm, the white shirt for me.

GIRL #3: (*os*) No—look at the one with the black pants on.

>   *Cut to: ms—*BILLY, GEORGE *and* WYATT *seated at table—woman proprietor bg behind counter.*

GEORGE: (*Mutters indistinctly.*)

BILLY: What did you say?

GEORGE: I said (*makes noise with tongue*), poontang!

>   *Cut to: cs—*BILLY—GIRLS *bg Left in booth—*DEPUTY *bg Right in booth.*

BILLY: (*Makes noise with tongue.*) What?

>   *Cut to: cs—*GEORGE.

GEORGE: (*Makes noise with tongue.*) Poontang!

>   *Cut to: cs—*BILLY—GIRLS *and* DEPUTY *in bg.*

BILLY: (*Makes noise with tongue.*) Poontang!

>   *Cut to: cs—*WYATT—*woman behind counter.*

GIRL #4: (*os*) Oh, I just—

>   *Cut to: mcs—three* GIRLS *seated Left in booth.*

GIRL #4: —can't believe—what are they doing here?

GIRL #5: Look at the teeth around his neck.

GIRL #6: Did they drive up on motorcycles?

Cut to: mcs—three GIRLS *seated Right in booth.*

GIRL #1: They know we're talking about them. They're looking over here.

*Cut to: cs—*BILLY *looking bg to* GIRLS *in booth—*DEPUTY *bg Right.*

GIRLS: (*Ad lib giggles.*)

BILLY *turns fg.*

BILLY: Hot damn! Ha! I tell you—

GEORGE: (*os*) I think—

*Cut to: cs—*GEORGE.

GEORGE: —I'll order kidneys, 'cause I left mine out there on the road somewhere.

*Cut to: cs—*WYATT.

BILLY: (*os*) (*Laughs.*)

Cut to: mcs—three GIRLS *seated Left in booth.*

GIRL #5: I don't know, but I like his hair all down his head.

GIRL #6: And I like his eyes.

*Cut to: cs—*GEORGE.

GEORGE: The girl right over there in the corner—

*Cut to: cs—*BILLY—GIRLS *and* DEPUTY *in bg—*BILLY *turns bg to look at* GIRLS.

*Cut to: cs—*GEORGE.

GEORGE: —well, don't look too close at her, because the sheriff is right over there.

*Cut to: cs—*BILLY—GIRLS *and* DEPUTY *in bg—*BILLY *turns to look bg at* DEPUTY.

GEORGE: (*os*) You know what I mean?

*Cut to: cs—*CAT MAN *in booth looking fg—*DEPUTY's *reflection in mirror.*

CAT MAN: Check that joker with the long hair.

DEPUTY: (*os*) I checked him already. Looks like we might have to bring him up to the Hilton before it's all over.

CAT MAN: Ha! I think she's cute.

DEPUTY: (*os*) Isn't she, though. I guess we'd put him in the women's cell, don't you reckon?

CAT MAN: Oh, I think we ought to put 'em in a cage and charge a little admission to see 'em.

*Cut to: cs—*GEORGE.

GEORGE: (*Sighs.*) Those are what is known as "country witticisms."

*Cut to: cs—*WYATT—*woman bg behind counter.*

GIRL #4: (*os*) Can't believe they're here. What are they doing here?

*Cut to: cs—*BILLY—GIRLS *and* DEPUTY *in bg—*BILLY *turns bg to look at* GIRLS.

GIRL #6: (*os*) I don't know.

GIRL #4: (*os*) Let's ask them to take us for a ride.

GIRL #6: (*os*) Oh, we can't—

Cut to: mcs—three GIRLS *Left in booth.*

GIRL #6: —ask them. Don't be a fool.

GIRL #5: Yeah.

GIRL #6: No. They'll think you're—Oh—They'll laugh in your face.

GIRL #5: Yeah. That'd be good, too.

GIRL #4: I doubt it.

GIRL #6: Oh, no.

GIRL #4: I'm gonna ask them.

GIRL #6: You might ask 'em.

GIRL #5: Not while I'm around you're not going to ask 'em.

GIRL #6: (*Overlap.*) Go ahead. Go ahead, ask 'em. I don't think you're gonna.

GIRL #5: Go ahead.

GIRL #4: Okay.

GIRL #6: Go on.

Ad lib giggles.

*Cut to: cs—*BILLY *looking bg Left at* GIRL*—*DEPUTY *bg Right—*MAN *bg partially hidden by* BILLY*—*BILLY *turns fg.*

CUSTOMER #1: You know, I thought at first that bunch over there, their mothers may have been frightened by a bunch of gorillas, but now I think they were caught.

*Cut to: cs—*WYATT—*woman in bg.*

CUSTOMER #2: (*os*) I know one of them is Alley-oop—I think. From the beads—

*Cut to: cs—*GEORGE.

CUSTOMER #2: (*os*) —on him.

CUSTOMER #4: (*os*) Well, one of them darned sure is not Oola.

CUSTOMER #1: (*os*) Look like a—

Cut to: mcs—two MEN *in booth.*

CUSTOMER #1: —bunch of refugees from a gorilla love-in.

CUSTOMER #2: A gorilla couldn't love that.

CUSTOMER #1: (*Laughs.*) Nor could a mother.

*Cut to: cs—*WYATT—*woman in bg.*
Ad lib laughter—os.
Cut to: ms—two men in booth.

CUSTOMER #3: Mate him up with one of those black wenches out there.

CUSTOMER #4: Oh, now I don't know about that.

CUSTOMER #3: Well, that's about as low as they come. I'll tell ya.

*Cut to: cs—*GEORGE.

GEORGE: Oh, he's a biggie.

Cut to: ms—two men in booth.

CUSTOMER #3: Man, they're green.

CUSTOMER #4: No, they're not green, they're white.

CUSTOMER #3: White? Huh!

Cut to: cs—BILLY—GIRL and DEPUTY in bg.

CUSTOMER #4: (*os*) Uh-huh.

CUSTOMER #3: (*os*) Man, then you're color blind. I just gotta say that.

BILLY: I'd sure like to get some food around here.

Cut to: cs—WYATT—woman in bg.

CUSTOMER #1: (*os*) I don't know, I thought most jails were built for humanity, and that won't quite qualify.

CUSTOMER #2: (*os*) I wonder—

Cut to: cs—DEPUTY.

CUSTOMER #2: (*os*) —where they got those wigs from.

CUSTOMER #1: (*os*) They probably—

Cut to: cs—GEORGE.

CUSTOMER #1: (*os*) —grew 'em. It looks like they're standin' in fertilizer.

Cut to: ms—woman proprietor standing behind counter.

CUSTOMER #1: (*os*) Nothin' else would grow on 'em.

Cut to: cs—GEORGE.

GEORGE: You know—uh—you know, I'm not real hungry at the moment. (*Laughs.*) You know what I mean?

Cut to: cs—WYATT—woman in bg.

CUSTOMER #3: (*os*) I saw—

Cut to: cs—MAN in booth—DEPUTY's reflection in mirror.

CUSTOMER #3: (*os*) —two of them one time. They were just—

Cut to: cs—DEPUTY.

CUSTOMER #3: (*os*) —kissin' away.

Cut to: two men in booth.

CUSTOMER #3: Two males. Just think of it.

Cut to: cs—WYATT—woman in bg.
Cut to: cs—BILLY—GIRL and DEPUTY in bg.
Cut to: cs—DEPUTY.

DEPUTY: What'cha think we ought to do with 'em?

Cut to: cs—CAT MAN—DEPUTY's reflection in mirror.

CAT MAN: I don't damn know, but I don't think they'll make the parish line.

> *Cut to: cs—*BILLY*—*GIRL *and* DEPUTY *in bg.*
>
> *Cut to: cs—*GEORGE*.*
>
> *Cut to: cs—*WYATT*—woman in bg.*

WYATT: Let's split.

BILLY: (*os*) Split?

WYATT: Yeah.

> *Cut to: cs—*BILLY*—*GIRL *and* DEPUTY *bg.*
>
> *Cut to: cs—*WYATT*—he rises.*
>
> *Cut to: cs—*GEORGE*—he rises.*
>
> *Cut to: cs—*MAN *in booth—*DEPUTY's *reflection in mirror.*
>
> *Cut to: mls—*GEORGE, WYATT *and* BILLY*—pan Left as they move bg to door.*

GEORGE: Yes, sir. It certainly has been nice.

> *Cut to: cs—*CAT MAN *in booth facing Right—* DEPUTY's *reflection in mirror.*

CAT MAN: They got some fancy bikes out there. That's some Yankee queers. Check the flag on that bike.

DEPUTY: (*os*) It sure is.

CAT MAN: I still say they're not gonna make the parish line.

> *Cut to: mls—ext restaurant—*BILLY *and* WYATT *on parked motorcycles—*GEORGE *standing by—*GIRLS *enter from restaurant.*

GEORGE: Here comes the p-p-p-poontang. (*Makes noise.*)

GIRLS: (*Ad lib.*) Hey, fellas, can we have a ride?

BILLY: You wanta ride?

GIRLS: (*Ad lib.*) Yeah, yeah. Please.

BOYS: (*Ad lib.*) You want a ride? You got a note from your mom?

GIRLS: Our mom? Oh, come on, please. Our mom won't mind. Please, let us have a ride.

Ad lib indistinct chatter.

BILLY: I don't mind giving you a ride. I'll give you a ride.

Ad lib indistinct chatter.

BILLY: The Man—the Man is at the window. The Man is at—

Cut to: ms—low angle: DEPUTY *and* MAN *looking fg out window.*

BILLY: (*os*) —the window. The Man is at the window.

*Cut to: mls—*GIRLS *gathered around* GEORGE, BILLY *and* WYATT—BILLY *and* WYATT *start up motorcycles.*

GIRLS: (*Ad lib.*) Oh, come on.

GEORGE: Oh, the Man is at the window.

Ad lib indistinct chatter.

Cut to: ms—low angle: DEPUTY *and* MAN *looking fg out window.*

140

Ad lib chatter.

Cut to: mls—BILLY and WYATT on cycles, backs to cam—GEORGE gets on behind WYATT—GIRLS move back.

GIRLS: (*Indistinct yells.*)

Cut to: ms—low angle: DEPUTY and MAN looking out window—they bend forward to look off Right.

Cut to: mls—GIRLS standing outside restaurant—DEPUTY and MAN seen through window.

Cut to: mls—ext campsite—night—low angle: trees —pan down to GEORGE, WYATT and BILLY on ground before open fire—hold mls.

Cut to: ms—GEORGE *and* BILLY.

Cut to: ms—WYATT.

GEORGE: (*os*) You know—

Cut to: cs—GEORGE.

GEORGE: —this used to be a helluva good country.

Cut to: mcs—BILLY *and* GEORGE—*favors* BILLY.

GEORGE: I can't understand what's gone wrong with it.

Cut to: mcs—GEORGE *and* BILLY—*favors* GEORGE.

BILLY: Huh. Man, everybody got chicken, that's what happened, man. Hey, we can't even get into—like—uh—second-rate hotels—

Cut to: mcs—BILLY *and* GEORGE—*favors* BILLY.

BILLY: I mean, a second-rate motel. You dig. They think we're gonna cut their throat or something, man. They're scared, man.

GEORGE: Oh, they're not scared of you. They're scared of what you represent to them.

BILLY: Hey, man. All we represent to them, man, is somebody needs a haircut.

GEORGE: Oh, no.

Cut to: mcs—GEORGE *and* BILLY—*favors* GEORGE.

GEORGE: What you represent to them is freedom.

BILLY: What the hell's wrong with freedom, man. That's what it's all about.

GEORGE: Oh, yeah; that's right—that's what it's all about, all right.

*Cut to: ms—*WYATT.

GEORGE: (*os*) But talking about it and being it—that's two different things.

Cut to: mcs—low angle: GEORGE *and* BILLY.

GEORGE: I mean, it's real hard to be free when you are bought and sold in the marketplace. 'Course don't ever tell anybody—

Cut to: mcs—low angle: GEORGE *and* BILLY—*favors* GEORGE.

GEORGE: —that they're not free, cause then they're gonna get real busy killin' and maimin' to prove to you that they are. Oh, yeah—they're gonna talk to you, and talk to you, and talk to you about individual freedom—

Cut to: mcs—low angle: BILLY *and* GEORGE—*favors* BILLY.

GEORGE: —but they see a free individual, it's gonna scare 'em.

BILLY: Mmmm, well, that don't make 'em runnin' scared.

Cut to: mcs—low angle: GEORGE *and* BILLY—*favors* GEORGE.

GEORGE: No. It makes 'em dangerous.

Cut to: mcs—low angle: BILLY *and* GEORGE—*favors* BILLY—GEORGE *flaps his arms.*

GEORGE: Nik, nik, nik, nik—

Cut to: ms—high angle: BILLY *and* GEORGE—GEORGE *flapping his arms.*

GEORGE: —nik, nik, nik, nik, nik—Swamp.

GEORGE *lies down, then leans up on elbows.*

GEORGE and BILLY: (*Ad lib snickers.*)

BILLY: (*Mutters.*) You're right, man. Whew. Swamp.

GEORGE: Swamp.

BILLY: Swamp.

> *Cut to: ms*—WYATT *lying on ground facing Right.*

BILLY: (*os*) Swamp?

GEORGE: (*os*) Swamp.

> *Cut to: ms*—GEORGE *and* BILLY.

GEORGE: Did ya ever—did ya ever talk to bullfrogs in the middle of the night?

BILLY: Not generally. (*Laughs.*)

GEORGE: You don't?

BILLY: No, man.

GEORGE: You know what I used to do?

BILLY: What did you used to do, man?

GEORGE: Well, I'll tell you one thing I didn't used to do is talk to bullfrogs in the middle of the night, you fool. (*Laughs.*)

BILLY: (*Laughs.*) You're out of your mind.

> GEORGE *shoves* BILLY *playfully.*
>
> *Cut to: ms*—WYATT *on ground facing Right—he puts his head down on helmet.*

GEORGE: (*os*) That's right.

> *Cut to: ls*—*ext campsite*—*night*—BILLY, GEORGE *and* WYATT *near smoldering fire wrapped in sleeping bags.*
>
> *Cut to: cs*—*high angle: smoldering fire*—*cam pans up Right to* WYATT *covered in sleeping bag—cam*

pans Right past him to mcs of GEORGE *sleeping—pair of legs move in—hand comes down with stick and hits at* GEORGE'S *head.*

Cut to: flash cuts of figures in sleeping bags—several men standing over beating at the three in sleeping bags— BILLY *sitting up bruised and bloody.*

Ad lib grunts.

BILLY: (*Yells.*)

Cut to: ms—high angle: BILLY *on ground bruised and bloody—* GEORGE'S *body Left in sleeping bag, his forehead bloody.*

BILLY: (*Yells—breathes hard.*)

Cut to: ms—high angle: BILLY *crouched over unconscious* WYATT*—he lifts him up and cradles him in his arms.*

BILLY: (*Ad lib sobs and mutters.*)

Cut to: mcs—high angle: WYATT, *his face bruised and bloody—* BILLY'S *hand in, slapping* WYATT'S *face.*

WYATT: (*Moans.*)

Cut to: ms—high angle: BILLY *kneeling over* WYATT.

BILLY: (*Mutters and breathes hard.*) Hey, man. Oh, man. Hey, man.

WYATT: (*Moans.*)

BILLY: Shhhh.

Cut to: mcs—high angle: GEORGE'S *body, blood on his face.*

147

Cut to: ms—high angle: BILLY *crouched down beside* WYATT, *knife in hand.*

BILLY: (*Breathes hard.*) Shhh-shhh.

Cut to: mcs—ext campsite—night—high angle: GEORGE's *sleeping bag, rip in it.*

BILLY: (*os*) O God, man! O God! (*Breathes hard.*)

Cam pulls back bringing in BILLY *and* WYATT *seated beside body—*BILLY *going through George's wallet.*

BILLY: What are we gonna do with his stuff, man, huh?

WYATT: Get it to his folks, somehow.

BILLY: There's not much here. There's some—there's some money in there and his driver's license, man. His—oh, man —here's his card, man. He ain't gonna be usin' that.

Cut to: cus—int New Orleans restaurant—night— hand·holding food over flame.

Cut to: cs—hand holding frying pan over fire.

*Cut to: cs—int restaurant—*WYATT *looking Right fg sadly.*

Music over—"Kyrie Eleison"

Cut to: cus—flickering lights—scene clears revealing cs WYATT *facing Right as he sips wine.*

*Cut to: cs—*WYATT *facing Right, sips wine.*

*Cut to: cus—*BILLY *facing fg, drags on cigarette.*

Cut to: mcs—high angle: hand holding two plates of food.

*Cut to: cs—*WYATT*—waiter's hand enters Left fg holding plate of food—pan down Right past* WYATT *to* BILLY's *hand taking plate.*

*Cut to: cs—*BILLY *facing Left, sips wine.*

Cut to: cus—WYATT *eating.*

BILLY: (*os*) Hey, no, really.

Cut to: ms—BILLY *and* WYATT *seated at table.*

BILLY: We'll go there for one drink, man, just one drink.

Cut to: cs—WYATT *looking down sadly.*
Cut to: cus—BILLY *eating.*
Cut to: cus—WYATT.
Cut to: cus—BILLY *sipping wine.*
Cut to: cs—WYATT *eating.*
Cut to: cus—BILLY.
Cut to: cus—WYATT.

BILLY: (*os*) No, man—hey, listen—now really—

Cut to: ms—BILLY *and* WYATT.

BILLY: —seriously now. He would have wanted us to, man.

Cut to: cs—WYATT *facing Left—flickering lights about him.*
Cut to: flash cuts of religious paintings.
Cut to: mcs—*int whorehouse*—BILLY *and* WYATT *looking upward.*
Cut to: mls—*low angle: ornate ceiling and chandelier —pan down to paintings on wall.*
Cut to: mcs—*religious paintings on wall.*
Cut to: cus—*painting of woman's breasts.*
Cut to: mcs—*int salon*—*two prostitutes seated on couch.*

149

Cut to: mls—int salon—girl dancing on table.

Cut to: ms—BILLY and WYATT in doorway.

Cut to: mcs—two PROSTITUTES seated on couch.

Cut to: ms—BILLY looking at group of prostitutes posing against wall.

Cut to: mcs—WYATT leaning against wall—pan Right as he crosses Right past MADAME, prostitute and pimp to painting on wall—stop and hold him mcs, back to cam.

Cut to: mcs—MADAME and prostitute—pimp behind them.

Cut to: mls—shooting from behind WYATT and BILLY to GIRL dancing on table—cam dollies in behind them as they cross room—BILLY pauses to pull open top of GIRL's dress.

Cut to: ms—prostitute seated on couch, legs apart.

Cut to: ms—shooting from behind BILLY *to* MADAME, *girl and man—*BILLY *turns fg.*

*Cut to: mcs—*WYATT *seated on couch—*GIRL *bg dancing on table.*

*Cut to: mls—*WYATT, BILLY *and two* PROSTITUTES *on couch—*GIRL *bg dancing on table.*

*Cut to: mcs—*WYATT *seated on couch looking fg bored—*GIRL *bg on table dancing.*

*Cut to: ms—*BILLY *snuggling up to two* PROSTITUTES.

*Cut to: mcs—*WYATT *leaning back on couch, eyes closed—*GIRL *bg at end of couch.*

*Cut to: ms—int private room—*BILLY *seated against wall drinking.*

*Cut to: mcs—*WYATT *standing looking up Left to wall, back to cam.*

WYATT: "If God did not exist it would be necessary to invent him."

BILLY: (*os*) (*Laughs.*) That's a humdinger.

WYATT *turns to look off Right.*
*Cut to: ms—*BILLY.

BILLY: Mmmm. I'm gettin' a little smashed.

*Cut to: mcs—*WYATT *facing Left—cam dollies back as he walks fg, running his fingers along inscription at base of mantel.*

BILLY: (*os*) Gettin' a little smashed.

WYATT *stops and leans his head against mantel.*

BILLY: (*os*) Yeah.

*Cut to: ms—*BILLY.

BILLY: Whew. Wow. It's hot in here, man. (*Sighs.*) Chicks.

*Cut to: mcs—*WYATT.

BILLY: (*os*) (*Sighs.*) Those chicks, man, those chicks.

Pan up Left past WYATT *to inscription on wall—it reads: Death only closes a man's reputation and determines it as good or bad.*

Cut to: quick flash: els—aerial shot: ext highway—fire burning alongside highway.

Cut to: mcs—int private room of whorehouse—

WYATT *looking up Left—pan Right bringing in* BILLY *seated bg fanning himself with his hat as* WYATT *crosses Right to chair and sits—*KAREN, MARY *and* MADAME *enter through door—*BILLY *rises.*

BILLY: Hey! Da-da— (*Mutters.*)

MADAME: Goodbye, girls. Later.

    MADAME *exits out door.*

BILLY: Howdy. Howdy.

MARY: Hello.

BILLY: My name is Billy. And this here is Captain America. Excuse me for one minute, ladies.

    BILLY *hurries fg to* WYATT.

*Cut to: mcs—*BILLY *leaning down to* WYATT.

BILLY: Man, do you mind if I take the tall one, man?

WYATT: No, that's all right.

BILLY: (*Mutters.*) Mmmmm.

> BILLY *leans up os.*
>
> *Cut to: mls—*BILLY *moves to* KAREN *and* MARY *and bows to* KAREN*—*WYATT *seated fg Right—*BILLY *and* KAREN *move bg to bench.*

BILLY: (*Mutters.*)

> *Cut to: cs—*WYATT *facing Left.*

BILLY: (*os*) Come on, you little hustler, you, get yourself over here. You old thing, you. I'm really from New York, you know. (*Laughs.*) You notice the Southern— (*Mutters.*)

> WYATT *turns and looks fg as* MARY *enters Left fg and sits down beside him.*

KAREN:ꞌ (*os*) You're a freak, aren't you.

> *Cut to: mcs—*MARY *and* WYATT*—favors* MARY.

MARY: My name is Mary.

> *Cut to: mcs—*WYATT *and* MARY*—favors* WYATT.

WYATT: Do you want a drink, Mary?

> *Cut to: mcs—*MARY *and* WYATT*—favors* MARY.

MARY: No, thanks.

154

KAREN: (os) Uh—what's—what's—uh—what's this?

    Focus on WYATT *as he faces Right.*

    *Cut to: ms—*KAREN *and* BILLY—*she fingers his long hair.*

KAREN: I mean, is this really your hair? (*Laughs.*)

    BILLY *fingers* KAREN's *hair.*

BILLY: Yeah, it really is. What is this? Is this really your hair? Are you kidding me?

    KAREN *fingers necklace around* BILLY's *neck.*

KAREN: Uh—what are these things?

    BILLY *points to* KAREN's *breasts.*

BILLY: Hey, what are these things?

KAREN: (*Laughs.*)

BILLY: (*Mutters.*)

KAREN: You know, I'm kind of a freak myself.

> *Cut to: cs—*WYATT *facing Right, takes off glasses—* MARY *in bg.*

BILLY: (*os*) Ha. I never really thought of myself as a freak. But I love to freak.

WYATT: What's happening outside?

> MARY *leans forward Right.*

MARY: What?

> *Cut to: mcs—shooting from behind* MARY *and* WYATT.

156

WYATT: You know, in the street. What's happening? Mardi
   Gras.

MARY: Oh, well—it's—you know—it's crowded and all that.

WYATT: Yeah.

      *Cut to: ms—*KAREN *and* BILLY.

BILLY: Mmmm—do you want a drink?

KAREN: Unh-unh.

BILLY: Mmmm. Here's to you.

KAREN: Thank you.

BILLY: (*Sighs.*)

      *Cut to: mcs—*MARY *and* WYATT—*favors* MARY.

MARY: What's the matter? Don't you like me?

WYATT: What?

MARY: Well, you paid for me, right?

      *Cut to: mcs—*WYATT *and* MARY—*favors* WYATT.

WYATT: Ohhh. That was—that was for my friend.

      *Cut to: mcs—*MARY *and* WYATT—*favors* MARY.

MARY: Oh. I don't—uh—

      *Cut to: mcs—*WYATT *and* MARY—*favors* WYATT.

WYATT: Why don't I buy you a drink?

*Cut to: mcs—*MARY *and* WYATT—*favors* MARY.

MARY: I don't drink.

Focus on WYATT *as he faces Right.*

WYATT: (*Sighs.*) I've got an idea.

Focus on MARY *as* WYATT *faces her.*
*Cut to: mcs—*WYATT *and* MARY—*favors* WYATT.

WYATT: Let's go outside.

WYATT *turns to look bg.*
*Cut to: ms—*BILLY *and* KAREN.

BILLY: Yep.

*Cut to: mcs—*WYATT *and* MARY—*favors* WYATT.

WYATT: We'll all go outside to Mardi Gras.

*Cut to: mcs—*MARY *and* WYATT—*favors* MARY.

MARY: Okay.

WYATT: Okay.

*Cut to: mcs—*WYATT *and* MARY—*favors* WYATT.

Cut to: mls—ext New Orleans—Mardi Gras time—
night—people in costumes parading in street.

Crowd noise.

Cut to: mls—people parading in street, carryin
torches. "When the Saints Go Marching In" plays i
bg throughout Mardi Gras sequence.

158

Cut to: ms—pan Right with man marching in street.

Cut to: ms—ext New Orleans street—cam dollies back as MARY *and* WYATT *walk fg followed by* BILLY *and* KAREN.

Cut to: mcs—pan Right with masked man parading in street.

Cut to: ms—cam dollies in behind MARY *and* WYATT *walking bg down street.*

Cut to: ms—low angle: masked man on float.

Cut to: ms—zoom up to mcs of masked man on horse.

*Cut to: ms—*WYATT, MARY, KAREN *and* BILLY *at food stand—they move fg.*

Cut to: mls—float moving bg down street.

Cut to: ms—cam dollies in behind KAREN *and* BILLY *as they hurry bg down sidewalk.*

Cut to: ms—two Negro men on street corner playing instruments.

Cut to: ms—pan Right as policemen hustle man across street.

Cut to: ms—cam dollies in behind KAREN, BILLY, MARY *and* WYATT *as they walk bg through arcade.*

Cut to: mls—low angle: float moving along street.

Cut to: ms—cam dollies back as MARY *and* WYATT *walk fg followed by* KAREN *and* BILLY—MARY *dances.*

Cut to: mcs—balloons.

*Cut to: mcs—*BILLY *and* KAREN *on street corner kissing.*

Cut to: mcs—boy carrying Negro doll on his shoulders.

Cut to: ms—Negro in Indian costume parading fg.

*Cut to: mcs—*KAREN *reaching out toward Indian headdress.*

Cut to: ls—day—low angle: sign on roof of hotel. The Roosevelt—float moves fg through scene.

Cut to: ms—cam dollies back as WYATT, BILLY *and* KAREN *walk fg—* MARY *follows.*

Cut to: ms—zoom up to float moving through scene.

Cut to: WYATT, BILLY *and* KAREN *walking fg—* MARY *follows.*

Cut to: mls—cam dollies in behind MARY, WYATT, KAREN *and* BILLY.

Cut to: mls—Home Guard marching fg—float in bg.

Cut to: mcs—American flag.

Cut to: mcs— WYATT, *back to cam—* MARY *in crowd bg.*

Cut to: mcs—two men in parade—crowd in bg.

Cut to: ms— WYATT, MARY, KAREN *and* BILLY *on sidewalk—they look upward—* BILLY *moves fg.*

Cut to: ms—low angle: float—zoom up to mcs.

Cut to: mcs— BILLY *looking up fg—others in bg.*

Cut to: mls—low angle: float.

Cut to: mcs— BILLY—*dolly in past him to mcs* MARY *and* WYATT.

Cut to: mcs—low angle: large doll in parade.

Cut to: ms—shooting from behind WYATT *to* Negro *with his hand on* BILLY'S *arm—* KAREN *and* MARY *behind Left—dolly in past* WYATT *to mcs Negro and* BILLY.

Cut to: ms—float of headless rider on horse.

Cut to: ms—cam dollies in behind MARY, WYATT, BILLY *and* KAREN *as they move bg down street.*

Cut to: mcs—Indian costumed men.

Cut to: mcs— WYATT *and* MARY *on street corner kissing—crowd gathered.*

Cut to: mls—low angle: oil derrick.

*Cut to: mls—*MARY, WYATT, KAREN *and* BILLY *on corner—oil derrick in bg—pan Right past* KAREN *and* BILLY *as* WYATT *and* MARY *hurry across street to Right.*

Cut to: ms—high angle: dead dog lying at curb.

*Cut to: ms—*MARY *and* WYATT *standing over dead dog—*WYATT *stoops down to it—*KAREN *and* BILLY *enter Left—*BILLY *stoops down to touch dog, draws his hand away and rises—*WYATT *rises—pan Right as they move bg down sidewalk.*

Cut to: mls—cemetery.

*Cut to: ms—ext cemetery—*MARY *walks fg and exits —*KAREN, BILLY *and* WYATT *bg approaching.*

Cut to: mls—cam dollies in along pathway—pan Left as cam dollies around onto another pathway.

Cut to: ms—pan Left as BILLY, KAREN, MARY *and* WYATT *move Left to crypt wall and sit on bench—* WYATT *holds out pills in his hand.*

BILLY: Hey!

KAREN: What's that?

BILLY: (*Laughs.*)

      BILLY *gets down on ground, back to cam.*

KAREN: What's that?

WYATT: Never mind. Just shut up and take it.

BILLY: Yeah, right.

      KAREN *kneels down beside* BILLY—BILLY *takes pill and puts it in his mouth—*WYATT *hands pill to* KAREN *and* MARY.

KAREN: What—what do you do with it?

WYATT: Give it to me.

BILLY: Just shut up and take it, man.

WYATT: Put it on your tongue.

> KAREN *takes pill, leans down and kisses* BILLY—
> WYATT *puts pill in* MARY's *mouth and one in his own
> —they kiss.*
>
> *Cut to: mls—low angle: crypt wall.*

GIRL'S VOICE: I believe in—

> *Cut to: ms—*BILLY *and* KAREN *on floor kissing—*
> MARY *and* WYATT *on bench.*

GIRL'S VOICE: —God,

> *Cut to: mls—low angle: crypt wall.*

GIRL'S VOICE: Father Almighty.

> *Cut to: ms—*KAREN *and* BILLY *embracing on ground
> —*WYATT *and* MARY *behind on bench.*
>
> *Cut to: mls—low angle: crypt wall.*

GIRL'S VOICE: Creator—

> *Cut to: ms—*KAREN *and* BILLY *on ground—*WYATT
> *and* MARY *on bench.*

GIRL'S VOICE: —of heaven and earth.

> MARY *drinks from bottle—*WYATT *kisses her.*

WYATT'S VOICE: (*Indistinct.*) The last—

Cut to: mls—low angle: crypt wall.

WYATT'S VOICE: —time—

    *Cut to: ms—*BILLY *and* KAREN *on ground—*WYATT *and* MARY *on bench.*

WYATT'S VOICE: —the last time—the last time.

    Cut to: mls—low angle: crypt wall.

    *Cut to: ms—the four—*BILLY *drinking from bottle.*

GIRL'S VOICE: Was cruci—

    Cut to: mls—low angle: crypt wall.

GIRL'S VOICE: —fied, died—

    Cut to: ms—the four.

GIRL'S VOICE: —and was buried. He descended into hell—

    Cut to: mls—low angle: crypt wall.

GIRL'S VOICE: —the third day He arose again from the dead. He ascended into heaven, to sitteth at the right hand of God —the Father Almighty.

    Cam pans Right to blazing sun.

WYATT: (*Overlaps.*) Oh, Mother, Mother, why didn't you tell me? Why didn't anybody tell me anything?

GIRL'S VOICE: Creator of heaven and earth.

    Cut to: cs—ext cemetery—day—low angle: GIRL.

GIRL: I believe in God, Father Almighty, creator—

WYATT'S VOICE: (*Indistinct.*) What are you doing to me—

> *Cut to: sun setting behind trees—zoom in and sun fills screen.*

GIRL'S VOICE: —of heaven and earth. And in Jesus Christ—

WYATT'S VOICE: (*Overlap.*) —Mother, what are you doing, Mother?

> *Cut to: cs—low angle:* GIRL.

GIRL: —his only son, Our Lord.

> *Cut to: mcs—low angle:* WYATT *pressing his face against that of a statue.*

WYATT: Shut up!

> *Cut to: mcs—telescopic view of man in cemetery.*
>
> *Cut to: mcs—low angle:* GIRL *moving Left carrying umbrella.*

GIRL'S VOICE: Received—

GIRL: (*Hums.*)

> *Cut to: ls—low angle: statue at top of dome.*

GIRL'S VOICE: —Holy Ghost.

> *Cut to: cs—cam pulls away from crucifix on cemetery vault.*

GIRL'S VOICE: Born of the Virgin Mary, suffered under Pontius Pilate—

Cut to: zoom back from moon.

GIRL'S VOICE: —was crucified, died and was buried.

Cut to: els—low angle: statues on domes—cam dollies in through cemetery.

GIRL'S VOICE: He descended into hell—

Cut to: mls—MARY in niche taking off her clothes.

GIRL'S VOICE: —the third day He arose—

Cut to: mls—telescopic view of MARY in nude, posing.

GIRL'S VOICE: —again from the dead—

Cut to: els—cam dollies through cemetery.

GIRL'S VOICE: —He ascended into heaven—

Cut to: mls—MARY in niche taking off clothes.

GIRL'S VOICE: —to sitteth at the right hand of God—

Cut to: mls—nude posing in cemetery.

Cut to: low angle: tree limbs silhouetted against sky as camera turns.

GIRL'S VOICE: —the Father Almighty. And then He shall come to judge the living and the dead. I believe in the Holy Ghost—

Cut to: ms—low angle: cam moving toward WYATT embracing statue.

WYATT: *(Sobs.)*

GIRL'S VOICE: —church.

      Cut to: ms—moving toward WYATT *embracing statue.*

WYATT: *(Sobs.)*

GIRL'S VOICE: The Communion—

      Cut to: ms—moving toward WYATT *embracing statue.*

GIRL'S VOICE: —of saints—

      Cut to: cs—cam pulls back from WYATT *posing with statue.*

WYATT: *(Indistinct.)*

GIRL'S VOICE: —the forgiveness of sins, the resurrection of the body—

      Cut to: ms—low angle: statue.

GIRL'S VOICE: —and—

      Cut to: mcs—low angle: flowers silhouetted against sky.

GIRL'S VOICE: —life—

      Cut to: ms—low angle: from rear of statue.

GIRL'S VOICE: —ever—

      Cut to: mcs—low angle: flowers silhouetted against sky.

GIRL'S VOICE: —lasting.

Cut to: ms—low angle: statue on pedestal.

WYATT'S VOICE: How could—

Cut to: ms—MARY in niche as she disrobes.

GIRL'S VOICE: Amen. Glory be to the Father and to the Son and to the Holy Ghost.

WYATT'S VOICE: —How could you make me hate you so?

GIRL'S VOICE: As it was in the beginning—

WYATT'S VOICE: Oh, God—

Cut to: cs—low angle: WYATT embracing statue.

WYATT: —I hate you so much.

GIRL'S VOICE: —is now and ever shall be. World without end. Amen.

Cut to: KAREN, nude, crouched in niche—BILLY crouched over her—WYATT standing in bg.

KAREN: Look at me.

BILLY: I want you to be beautiful.

KAREN: I always wanted to be pretty.

BILLY: I want you to be beautiful. No.

Cut to: mls—KAREN frolicking through cemetery.

BILLY'S VOICE: Shhhh.

Cut to: mls—KAREN, BILLY *and* WYATT *in niche.*

KAREN: (*Indistinct.*)

BILLY: Listen to me—listen to me.

Cut to: mls—KAREN *running fg.*

BILLY'S VOICE: I want you—

Cut to: mls—BILLY, KAREN *and* WYATT *in niche.*

BILLY: — to be beautiful.

Cut to: mls—KAREN *running fg.*

BILLY'S VOICE: I want you to be—

Cut to: mls—BILLY, KAREN *and* WYATT *in niche.*

BILLY'S VOICE: —beautiful.

Cut to: mls—KAREN *runs fg and halts in ms.*

KAREN'S VOICE: No. No.

Cut to: low angle: cam pans across sky.

KAREN'S VOICE: (*Sobs.*) I know you.

Cut to: indistinguishable movement in cemetery.

BILLY'S VOICE: Baby, baby—

KAREN'S VOICE: (*Sobs.*)

168

Cut to: rippling water.

Indistinct murmurs.

Come back.

Cut to: flashing light.

Indistinct murmurs.

Cut to: cam pans across cemetery buildings.

Indistinct murmurs.

KAREN'S VOICE: I know you.

Cut to: indistinguishable movement in cemetery.

Indistinct murmurs and moans.

Cut to: flickering lights.

Ad lib indistinct moans.

Cut to: cus—KAREN and BILLY embracing on ground.

Ad lib indistinct murmurs and moans.

KAREN: Hold my head back.

Cut to: shimmering lights.

Cut to: telescopic view of man in cemetery reading from document—WYATT in bg, intercut, bringing him close to man.

GIRL'S VOICE: Blessed art Thou amongst women, and blessed—

Cut to: flash cuts: indistinguishable movement in cemetery—WYATT embracing statue—WYATT and MARY, nude, embracing in crypt—crypt wall—WYATT on ledge holding umbrella—KAREN and BILLY kissing.

GIRL'S VOICE: —is the fruit of Thy womb, Jesus.

WYATT'S VOICE: Make me love you.

*Cut to: cs—*WYATT—*pan up to his upraised hand.*

GIRL'S VOICE: Holy Mary, Mother of God, pray for us now—

*Cut to: mls—*KAREN *in niche pawing at wall—*WYATT *in bg.*

KAREN: I know it. I know you. I know you. I know you.

Cut to: flash shots of Mardi Gras parade.

*Cut to: ms—low angle: boy and girl at altar—*BILLY *enters fg and staggers bg between them.*

BILLY: (*Ad lib indistinct mutters.*)

Cut to: flash cuts of Mardi Gras parade and flashing lights.

BILLY'S VOICE: (*Ad lib laughter and mutters.*)

GIRL'S VOICE: —In the name of the Father—

*Cut to: cus—*KAREN—BILLY'*s hands on her face.*

Cut to: ornate grillwork.

BILLY'S VOICE: I'm all aglow—

*Cut to: cs—*WYATT *looking up Left.*

BILLY'S VOICE: —man.

Cut to: ornate grillwork.

BILLY'S VOICE: We're gonna—

*Cut to: cs.—*WYATT *looking up Left.*

BILLY'S VOICE: We're all aglow—

Cut to: ornate grillwork.

BILLY'S VOICE: Look—glow.

*Cut to: cs—*WYATT *looking up Left.*

BILLY'S VOICE: Glow.

Cut to: cs—iron cross—cam pulls back.

BILLY'S VOICE: Glow. Look—glow.

Cut to: ms—low angle: KAREN *seated—*BILLY *standing Left fg below drinking from bottle.*

KAREN: I know who you are. You're a John. I don't know why I like you.

VOICE: (*Overlap—indistinct.*)

*Cut to: ms—*KAREN *posing as she pulls up hose.*

Cut to: ms—low angle: KAREN *seated—*BILLY *standing Left fg below.*

KAREN: I don't even know if I like you.

BILLY: I know why I like you. (*Laughs.*)

*Cut to: ms—*KAREN *posing as she pulls up hose.*

BILLY'S VOICE: I know why I like you.

Cut to: ms—low angle: KAREN *and* BILLY.

BILLY: (*Laughs.*)

> *Cut to: cus—*KAREN *and* BILLY *in passionate embrace.*

KAREN: (*Screams.*)

> *Cut to: cus—*KAREN's *legs.*

KAREN: (*Screams.*)

> *Cut to: cus—*BILLY *holding* KAREN *os.*

KAREN: (*os*) Don't you—

> *Cut to: cus—*KAREN's *head thrown back, mouth open.*

KAREN: —dare. (*Laughs.*)

> *Cut to: cus—open palm.*

KAREN: (*os*) Don't you—

> *Cut to: cus—*BILLY *holding* KAREN *os.*

KAREN: (*os*) —dare.

> *Cut to: cus—high angle:* KAREN's *face passive, eyes closed.*

KAREN: (*Gasps.*)

> *Cut to: mls—cam dollies in along crypt wall.*

MARY'S VOICE: I can feel the outside. I can feel the outside—but I can't—I can't—I can't feel the inside. Okay?

Cut to: mls—cam pans Right along cemetery build-ings.

KAREN'S VOICE: Don't stop! Don't stop!

BILLY'S VOICE: Shhhh-shhhh.

Cut to: mls—high angle: MARY, nude, being held by WYATT as they crouch on grave.

MARY: I'm dying!

WYATT: No.

Cut to: ms—low angle: hand tossing umbrella—pan with it.

MARY'S VOICE: I'm going to die.

Cut to: mls—cam panning across cemetery.

MARY'S VOICE: I'm going to die.

Cut to: mls—cam panning across cemetery.

MARY'S VOICE: (*Screams.*)

Cut to: mls—WYATT standing in between walls of crypts, back to cam.

MARY'S VOICE: (*Ad lib sobbing.*) I'm dead.

Cut to: ms—MARY, nude, hanging out from niche in wall.

MARY'S VOICE: (*Ad lib sobbing.*) I'm dead.

Cut to: ms—KAREN *and* BILLY *kissing passionately—* WYATT *seated bg in corner of grave holding* MARY, *nude.*

MARY'S VOICE: Do you understand?

Cut to: mls—low angle: WYATT *holding out umbrella —cam dollies in Left and pans Right.*

WYATT'S VOICE: (*Singing.*) "Mary loves John loves, Mary loves—"

Cut to: els—shooting through archway to umbrella.

WYATT'S VOICE: (*Sings.*) "—John loves—"

Cut to: ls—cam panning across cemetery.

MARY'S VOICE: (*Sobs.*) Oh, dear God, please let it be. Please—

Cut to: mls—low angle: indistinguishable figure on statue.

MARY'S VOICE: —help—

Cut to: cus—flames leaping up from gas jet.

MARY'S VOICE: —me conceive—

Cut to: cus—large billowing object.

MARY'S VOICE: —a child.

Cut to: flash of light.
Cut to: els—telescopic view of cemetery.

MARY'S VOICE: I'm right out here.

Cut to: ms—telescopic view of man with umbrella—
he runs bg.

MARY'S VOICE: I'm right out here. I'm right out here.

*Cut to: mcs—*KAREN *in niche facing Left—move in*
to cs.

MARY'S VOICE: I'm right out here—out of my—

Cut to: cam panning across cemetery.

MARY'S VOICE: —head.

Cut to: ms—low angle: statue.

GIRL'S VOICE: And—

Cut to: mls—low angle: statue.

GIRL'S VOICE: —in—

Cut to: ms—low angle: back of statue.

GIRL'S VOICE: —Jesus—

*Cut to: mls—*MARY *and* WYATT *seated against tomb-*
stone.

GIRL'S VOICE: —Christ—

Cut to: mls—matte shot: MARY *nude rising from*
ground.

MARY'S VOICE: *(Yells indistinctly.)*

*Cut to: mls—*MARY *and* WYATT *against tombstone.*

GIRL'S VOICE: —Our Lord.

Cut to: flashing shots of light, statues and iron cross.

MARY'S VOICE: Please God, let me out of—

Cut to: ms—low angle: hand pushing up on grille.

MARY'S VOICE: —here.

Cut to: mls—high angle: MARY *lying face down on ground, nude.*

MARY'S VOICE: *(Sobs.)*

GIRL'S VOICE: —suffered under Pontius Pilate—

*Cut to: mls—*MARY *and* WYATT *in niche.*

MARY: *(Sobs.)* I want to get out of here. *(Sobs.)*

*Cut to: ms—*BILLY *and* KAREN *seated—*WYATT *and* MARY, *nude, bg in embrace.*

KAREN: You know what I mean.

MARY: *(Sobs.)*

*Cut to: ms—*KAREN *crouched in niche—*BILLY *in bg.*

KAREN: You wanted me.

*Cut to: ms—*KAREN *and* BILLY*—*WYATT *and* MARY *in bg.*

176

BILLY: *(Laughs.)*

> *Cut to: flashing light.*

> *Cut to: ms—*KAREN *and* BILLY—WYATT *and* MARY *in bg.*

KAREN: You know what I mean?

> *Cut to: ms—*KAREN *crouched in niche—*BILLY *behind.*

KAREN: You know what I mean?

> *Cut to: cam pans across flashing lights.*

KAREN'S VOICE: You wanted me ugly—

> *Cut to: matte shot of gate swinging open and shut.*

KAREN'S VOICE: —didn't you? I know you johns—I know you johns.

> *Cut to: indistinguishable flash cuts.*

WYATT'S VOICE: I hate you so much.

GIRL'S VOICE: In the name of the Father, and of the Son, and of—

> *Cut to: mcs—low angle:* WYATT *embracing statue.*

GIRL'S VOICE: —the Holy Spirit.

WYATT'S VOICE: You never loved me.

GIRL'S VOICE: Amen. I believe in God, the Father Almighty—

WYATT'S VOICE: Why did you leave like that?

GIRL'S VOICE: *(Overlap.)* —Creator of heaven and earth.

*Cut to: ms—matte shot: man reading Bible at grave-side—*WYATT *stoops down behind him.*

WYATT'S VOICE: Everybody else—but not you.

GIRL'S VOICE: Crucified, died and was buried. He descended into hell—

Cut to: moon in sky.

WYATT'S VOICE: And not me.

GIRL'S VOICE: —the third day He arose. Hallowed be Thy Name.

WYATT'S VOICE: I loved you.

Cut to: mls—low angle: crypt wall.
Cut to: moon brought closer.

GIRL'S VOICE: Thy kingdom come—

WYATT'S VOICE: I loved you—

Cut to: mls—low angle: crypt wall.

GIRL'S VOICE: —Thy will be done—

Cut to: moon brought closer.

GIRL'S VOICE: —on earth—

Cut to: mls—low angle: crypt wall.

WYATT'S VOICE: Oh, God how I loved you, Mother.

GIRL'S VOICE: —as it is in heaven. Give us this day our daily—

    Cut to: moon brought closer.

GIRL'S VOICE: —bread. And forgive us our trespasses—

    Cut to: mls—low angle: crypt wall.

WYATT'S VOICE: And you're such a *fool* mother—and I hate you so much.

GIRL'S VOICE: —as we forgive—

    Music over—"Flash, Bam, Pow."

    Cut to: flash pan.

    Cut to: flash cuts: traveling shots of countryside, towns and buildings.

    Cut to: ms—ext bridge—day—cam trucks back Right as BILLY and WYATT ride Right across bridge on motorcycles.

Cut to: mcs—cam trucks back holding on WYATT's
helmet tied to sissy-bar.

Cut to: ms—cam trucks in Left behind WYATT *and*
BILLY *riding Left past barrier with sign: ROAD
CLOSED—columns in bg.*

Cut to: ls—cam trucking Left holding on plantation.

Cut to: ms—cam trucks back Right as WYATT *and*
BILLY *ride to Right—pipes and oil drums bg in field.*

Cut to: mls—cam trucks back as BILLY *and* WYATT
ride fg on road, crossing RR tracks.

*Cut to: ls—low angle: steel girders—pan down bring-
ing in* WYATT *and* BILLY *traveling bg across bridge—
truck in behind them.*

*Cut to: mls—low angle: trucking Left past trees with
sun flickering through branches.*

*Cut to: mcs—ext campsite—night—*WYATT *seated on
ground, staring down Left.*

WYATT: *(Sighs.)*

*Cut to: mcs—ext campsite—*BILLY *seated looking
Left fg.*

*Cut to: mcs—*WYATT.

*Cut to: mcs—*BILLY.

*Cut to: mcs—*WYATT.

BILLY: *(os) (Laughs.)* We've done it. We've—

*Cut to: mcs—*BILLY.

BILLY: —done it. We're rich, Wyatt. *(Laughs.)* Yeah, man.
(Laughs.) Yeah.

*Cut to: mls—*BILLY *and* WYATT *Left before open fire.*

BILLY: Yeah, we did it, man we did it. We did it. Huh. We're rich, man. We're retired in Florida, now, mister. *(Sighs— chuckles.)* Whew.

WYATT: You know, Billy—

> *Cut to: mcs—*WYATT.

WYATT: —we blew it.

> *Cut to: mcs—*BILLY *lying down—he sits up Right.*

BILLY: What? Huh? Wha-wha-wha— That's what it's all about, man. I mean, like you know—I mean, you go for the big money, man—and then you're free. You dig? *(Laughs.)*

> *Cut to: mcs—*WYATT.

WYATT: We blew it.

> *Cut to: mcs—*BILLY *frowns.*
>
> *Cut to: mcs—*WYATT—*he turns bg and settles down on bedroll.*

WYATT: Good night, man.

> *Cut to: mcs—pan down Left as* BILLY *lies back.*
>
> *Cut to: mcs—*WYATT *lying down, back to cam.*

WYATT: *(Sighs.)*

> *Cut to: mls—travel shot through small town.*
>
> *Cut to: mcs—ext campsite—night—*WYATT *sleeping, back to cam.*
>
> *Cut to: els—ext road—cam trucks in along long stretch of road.*

*Cut to: mcs—ext campsite—night—*WYATT *sleeping, back to cam.*

Cut to: els—day—long stretch of road.

*Cut to: ls—ext road—*BILLY *and* WYATT *traveling bg.*

Cut to: mls—truck back as WYATT *and* BILLY *ride fg on motorcycles.*

Cut to: flash cuts: WYATT *and* BILLY *traveling fg and bg down road.*

Cut to: mls—cam trucks Left holding on building on stilts.

Cut to: els—cam trucks in along long stretch of road.

*Cut to: els—*BILLY *and* WYATT *traveling bg.*

Music over—"It's Alright, Ma (I'm Only Bleeding.)"

Cut to: els—long stretch of road.

Cut to: ls—travel shot: by gas station.

Cut to: ls—cam trucks Left holding on river—RR train bg.

Cut to: els—long stretch of road.

Cut to: ls—river and train.

Cut to: ls—trucking in behind WYATT *and* BILLY *traveling bg down road.*

Cut to: mls—travel shot: by gas station.

Cut to: ms—high angle: travel shot: motorcycle wheels moving Right.

Cut to: ms—cam trucks back Right as WYATT *and* BILLY *travel Right.*

Cut to: ms—high angle: travel shot: rear tires of cycle moving Right, exit revealing second cycle.

Cut to: ms—cam trucks in behind WYATT *and* BILLY *traveling bg.*

Cut to: ms—cam trucks Right as BILLY *and* WYATT

travel Right.

Cut to: ms—cam trucks in Right as BILLY *and* WYATT *travel bg Right.*

Cut to: ms—cam trucks in Right as BILLY *and* WYATT *travel bg Right.*

Cut to: ms—cam trucks back Right as WYATT *and* BILLY *travel Right fg.*

Cut to: ms—cam trucks back Right as WYATT *and* BILLY *travel Right.*

Cut to: ms—cam trucks back as BILLY *and* WYATT *travel fg.*

Cut to: els—long stretch of highway—car approaches—cam trucks in and pans Left, bringing in WYATT *and* BILLY *traveling fg along highway.*

Cut to: els—cam trucks Left over bridge holding on shipyard in bg.

*Cut to: mls—*BILLY *and* WYATT *travel bg along highway.*

Cut to: els—cam trucks Left over bridge, holding on shipyard bg.

*Cut to: mls—*BILLY *and* WYATT *traveling bg.*

Cut to: els—cam trucks Left over bridge, holding on shipyard bg.

Cut to: mls—truck in behind WYATT *and* BILLY *traveling bg.*

Cut to: mls—truck back as the two travel fg.

*Cut to: mls—*BILLY *and* WYATT *traveling bg.*

*Cut to: mls—*WYATT *and* BILLY *travel fg.*

Cut to: els—cam trucks Left along highway, holding onto river with thick wooded area in bg.

Cut to: cam trucks Right along road and zooms in to brush along highway.

*Cut to: mls—cam trucks Right along highway, holding onto countryside—*WYATT *rides in Left—pan Right and truck in behind him as he travels bg down highway—*BILLY *enters fg and follows.*

Cut to: ms—ext moving pickup—day—shooting through windshield at DRIVER *Right—*ROY *Left beside him.*

DRIVER: Hey, Roy, look at them ginks!

ROY: Pull alongside, we'll scare the hell out of 'em.

ROY *reaches back and takes down shotgun.*

Cut to: mls—ext road—cam trucks in behind BILLY *—*WYATT *bg ahead—pan Right past* WYATT *to ms of* BILLY *traveling Left.*

*Cut to: mcs—ext pickup—*ROY *aiming shotgun fg out window—*DRIVER *in bg.*

ROY: Want me to blow your brains out?

> *Cut to: ms—shooting from* ROY's *pov to* BILLY *traveling Left—*BILLY *looks fg and gives "finger."*
>
> *Cut to: mcs—*ROY *aiming shotgun fg out window—*DRIVER *in bg.*

ROY: Why don't you get a haircut?

> *Cut to: ms—cam trucks Left as* BILLY *travels Left.*
>
> *Cut to: ms—cam trucks Right as pickup travels Right—*ROY *aiming shotgun out window—he fires.*
>
> *Cut to: ls—ext road—*BILLY *falls off cycle to side of road—cycle skids fg.*
>
> *Cut to: ms—cam trucks Right as pickup travels Right—*ROY *seen through side window looking bg to* DRIVER.

DRIVER: What happened?

*Cut to: ls—*BILLY *rolls to side of road—cycle comes to halt in road.*

Cut to: mls—cam trucks in toward WYATT *stopped on road—pan Right to him and move by.*

*Cut to: mls—*BILLY's *overturned cycle on road—* BILLY *lying bg at side of road.*

*Cut to: mls—*WYATT *travels fg to ms and turns Right.*

Cut to: ms—ext moving pickup—shooting through windshield at ROY *and* DRIVER.

*Cut to: mls—ext road—*WYATT *gets off cycle—pan Right as he hurries Right and enters to* BILLY *lying bleeding at side of road—stop and hold mls as* WYATT *kneels down to him.*

WYATT: Billy!

BILLY: Oh, my God! *(Gags.)*

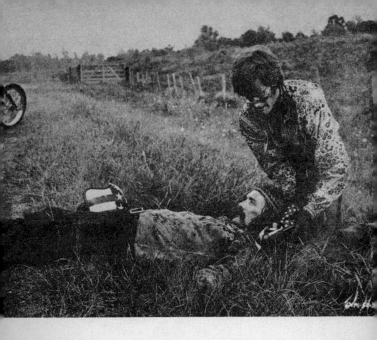

WYATT: Oh, my God! I'm going for help, Billy.

BILLY: I got 'em. I'm gonna get 'em. *(Sobs.)*

> WYATT *rises.*
>
> *Cut to: ms—ext moving pickup—shooting through windshield at* ROY *and* DRIVER.

ROY: We'd better go back.

> *Cut to: mls—ext road—*BILLY *lying Right at side of road—*WYATT *Left at cycle—he takes jacket from sissy-bar—pan Right as he runs Right to* BILLY *and covers him—hold the two mls.*

BILLY: *(Moans.)* Man, I—I'm gonna get 'em. Where are they now?

Pan Left as WYATT *runs bg to cycle—he gets on and travels bg down road.*

Cut to: ls—cam trucks in as pickup makes turn in road.

*Cut to: ls—*WYATT *approaches on cycle.*

Cut to: ls—cam trucks in as pickup approaches.

*Cut to: mls—*WYATT *travels Left fg.*

Cut to: ms—pickup traveling Left, DRIVER *seen through window—gunfire through window.*

Cut to: flash scene.

Cut to: ms—motorcycle flies fg into scene.

Cut to: mls—motorcycle flying through air, wheel falls off—cycle hits ground.

Cut to: mls—motorcycle bursts into flames.

Cut to: aerial shot: burning motorcycle.

Cut to: ms—motorcycle on ground burning.

Cut to: ls—aerial shot: burning motorcycle at edge of road—copter pulls up to hold els.

Music over—"Ballad of Easy Rider."

Fade in superimposed roll-up credits.

In order of appearance:

WYATT	*PETER FONDA*
BILLY	*DENNIS HOPPER*
JESUS	*ANTONIO MENDOZA*
THE CONNECTION	*PHIL SPECTOR*
BODYGUARD	*MAC MASHOURIAN*
RANCHER	*WARREN FINNERTY*
RANCHER'S WIFE	*TITA COLORADO*
STRANGER ON HIGHWAY	*LUKE ASKEW*

COMMUNE:	
LISA	*LUANA ANDERS*
SARAH	*SABRINA SCHARF*
JOANNE	*SANDY WYETH*
JACK	*ROBERT WALKER*
MIME #1	*ROBERT BALL*
MIME #2	*CARMEN PHILLIPS*
MIME #3	*ELLIE WALKER*
MIME #4	*MICHAEL PATAKI*

JAIL:	
GEORGE HANSON	*JACK NICHOLSON*
GUARD	*GEORGE FOWLER, JR.*
SHERIFF	*KEITH GREEN*

CAFE:	
CAT MAN	*HAYWARD ROBILLARD*
DEPUTY	*ARNOLD HESS, JR.*
CUSTOMER #1	*BUDDY CAUSEY, JR.*
CUSTOMER #2	*DUFFY LAFONT*
CUSTOMER #3	*BLASE M. DAWSON*
CUSTOMER #4	*PAUL GUEDRY, JR.*
GIRL #1	*SUZIE RAMAGOS*
GIRL #2	*ELIDA ANN HEBERT*
GIRL #3	*ROSE LeBLANC*
GIRL #4	*MARY KAYE HEBERT*

| GIRL #5 | CYNTHIA GREZAFFI |
| GIRL #6 | COLETTE PURPERA |

HOUSE OF BLUE
  LIGHTS:

MARY	TONI BASIL
KAREN	KAREN BLACK
MADAME	LEA MARMER
DANCING GIRL	CATHE COZZI
HOOKER #1	THEA SALERNO
HOOKER #2	ANNE McCLAIN
HOOKER #3	BEATRIZ MONTEIL
HOOKER #4	MARCIA BOWMAN

| PICKUP TRUCK: | DAVID C. BILLODEAU |
| | JOHNNY DAVID |

PERFORMER — TITLE — COMPOSER

STEPPENWOLF
  "THE PUSHER"   HOYT AXTON
STEPPENWOLF
  "BORN TO BE   MARS BONFIRE
    WILD"
THE BYRDS
  "WASN'T BORN TO   GERRY GOFFIN
    FOLLOW"   and CAROLE KING
THE BAND
  "THE WEIGHT"   JAIME ROBBIE
                    ROBERTSON
THE HOLY MODAL
ROUNDERS
  "IF YOU WANT TO   ANTONIA DUREN
    BE A BIRD"
FRATERNITY OF MAN
  "DON'T BOGART   ELLIOTT INGBER
    ME"   and LARRY WAGNER
THE JIMI HENDRIX
EXPERIENCE
  "IF SIX WAS NINE" JIMI HENDRIX
LITTLE EVA
  "LET'S TURKEY   GERRY GOFFIN
    TROT"   and JACK KELLER
THE ELECTRIC PRUNES
  "KYRIE ELEISON"   DAVID AXELROD

THE ELECTRIC FLAG,
AN AMERICAN MUSIC
BAND
  "FLASH, BAM,   MIKE BLOOMFIELD
      POW"
ROGER McGUINN
  "IT'S ALRIGHT MA   BOB DYLAN
      (I'M ONLY
      BLEEDING)"
ROGER McGUINN
  "BALLAD OF
      EASY RIDER"   ROGER McGUINN

Cam has panned away from wreckage to els aerial shot of lake.

Fade out.

SIGNET and **MENTOR** Books of Special Interest